THE SHIP OF LOVE

In silence Rowena walked back to her prison cell. It was a relief when she could be alone again and face the shattering thoughts that had overtaken her.

She would never beg for the Sultan's love, because he was not, and never could be, the man she loved.

The man she loved was Mark.

It was Mark.

It had always been Mark.

How long had she been in love with him and refused to admit it to herself?

Perhaps from the first evening when he had made her so angry, yet left her with a strange feeling of excitement. He had thrilled her even when she had thought she disliked him.

And then they had met again, in the woods, and she had sensed his power even when she rebelled against it. Her heart and her instincts had known then that the man she loved must be strong, as this man was strong.

The Barbara Cartland Pink Collection

Titles in this series

THE SHIP OF LOVE

BARBARA CARTLAND

Barbaracartland.com Ltd

THE BARBARA CARTLAND PINK COLLECTION

Barbara Cartland was the most prolific bestselling author in the history of the world. She was frequently in the Guinness Book of Records for writing more books in a year than any other living author. In fact her most amazing literary feat was when her publishers asked for more Barbara Cartland romances, she doubled her output from 10 books a year to over 20 books a year, when she was 77.

She went on writing continuously at this rate for 20 years and wrote her last book at the age of 97, thus completing 400 books between the ages of 77 and 97.

Her publishers finally could not keep up with this phenomenal output, so at her death she left 160 unpublished manuscripts, something again that no other author has ever achieved.

Now the exciting news is that these 160 original unpublished Barbara Cartland books are ready for publication and they will be published by Barbaracartland.com exclusively on the internet, as the web is the best possible way to reach so many Barbara Cartland readers around the world.

The 160 books will be published monthly and will be

numbered in sequence.

The series is called the Pink Collection as a tribute to Barbara Cartland whose favourite colour was pink and it became very much her trademark over the years.

The Barbara Cartland Pink Collection is published only on the internet. Log on to www.barbaracartland.com to find out how you can purchase the books monthly as they are published, and take out a subscription that will ensure that all subsequent editions are delivered to you by mail order to your home.

If you do not have access to a computer you can write for information about the Pink Collection to the following address :

Barbara Cartland.com Ltd.

240 High Road,

Harrow Weald,

Harrow HA3 7BB

United Kingdom.

Telephone & fax: +44 (0)20 8863 2520

THE LATE DAME BARBARA CARTLAND

Barbara Cartland who sadly died in May 2000 at the age of nearly 99 was the world's most famous romantic novelist who wrote 723 books in her lifetime with worldwide sales of over 1 billion copies and her books were translated into 36 different languages.

As well as romantic novels, she wrote historical biographies, 6 autobiographies, theatrical plays, books of advice on life, love, vitamins and cookery. She also found time to be a political speaker and television and radio personality.

She wrote her first book at the age of 21 and this was called *Jigsaw*. It became an immediate bestseller and sold 100,000 copies in hardback and was translated into 6 different languages. She wrote continuously throughout her life, writing bestsellers for an astonishing 76 years. Her books have always been immensely popular in the United States, where in 1976 her current books were at numbers 1 & 2 in the B. Dalton bestsellers list, a feat never achieved before or since by any author.

Barbara Cartland became a legend in her own lifetime and will be best remembered for her wonderful romantic novels, so loved by her millions of readers throughout the world.

Her books will always be treasured for their moral message, her pure and innocent heroines, her good looking and dashing heroes and above all her belief that the power of love is more important than anything else in everyone's life.

"The sea can be so beautiful. It stretches from horizon to horizon and goes on forever just like the real true love of a man and a woman for each other."

Barbara Cartland

CHAPTER ONE
1877

"I shall die of love for you! I know I shall. Dearest, most beautiful Rowena, goddess of my heart, say you return just a fraction of my adoration and I ask no more."

The young man seemed about to expire from passion, but instead of impressing Rowena Thornhill it only made her want to laugh.

He was rather plump, and not at all the right shape for declarations of eternal love.

"Do get up, Sir Cedric," she said, struggling to free her hand. "And let me go."

"Not until you say you're mine," he moaned.

"Well, I'm not yours and I'm never going to be."

"Adorable, loveliest Rowena – "

"My name is Miss Thornhill, and if you don't get up I shall scream."

That made him rise reluctantly, but still he clung to her hand until she rapped his knuckles with her fan.

Miss Rowena Thornhill was almost nineteen with a soft, peach like skin and golden hair that hung in soft curls around her heart shaped face.

In her pink lace and satin ball gown, she looked glorious enough to inspire any man with love, but Sir

Cedric's debts were notorious, and she knew that it was her father's bank balance, rather than her own charms, that had caused these ecstasies.

The knowledge didn't break her heart, for she cared nothing for Sir Cedric. But it was depressing. She would have liked to be appreciated for herself.

Normally she enjoyed balls, but she wished she'd never come to this one. It was almost the last dance of the season, and everyone who was still in London was there.

Lights blazed from the windows, the finest food and wines were served by powdered footmen, and all about her attractive men and women laughed, danced and flirted.

But Rowena was beginning to find these occasions troubling. They had an atmosphere that disturbed her.

Gradually she'd realised that nobody looked at her without calculating that her father was one of the richest men in England.

She was looking forward to escaping London for the peace and honesty of the country.

But first she had to deal with this unimpressive swain.

"Don't play with my feelings," he begged. "I adore you madly."

"And I tell you that I don't adore you, and never could."

"After the encouragement you gave me – "

"I did no such thing!"

"You left the ball with me."

"I left with you because you were making such a fuss and people were beginning to stare. But now I'm going back."

Desperation gave her callow admirer courage. Swooping suddenly, he tried to put his arms about her and kiss her.

"How dare you!" she exclaimed furiously. "Release me at once."

Instead of obeying he made another attempt to reach her mouth, breathing wine fumes all over her.

That was enough to make Miss Thornhill lose her temper. The next moment Sir Cedric was clutching his cheek, that smarted under a very unladylike slap

"And I'll do it again if you don't stop being so silly," she said breathlessly.

Then, turning, she fled.

She'd never been in Ellesmere House before, so she simply headed as far from the ballroom as possible, anxious to get away from the sound of music.

But Sir Cedric was coming after her. She ran harder, lost now and with no idea where she was going. The house was ablaze with lights for this was the final ball of the season, and nothing had been spared to show it off at its finest.

Then she opened a door at random, and found herself in a room without lights. All she could see were the great French windows leading to the moonlit garden.

Once out there she might be lost among the trees. Just one final burst of speed towards the open windows –

But suddenly she collided hard with a human form, and a man's voice said impatiently,

"Be careful."

In the semi darkness she could make out a tall man with broad shoulders. His voice was strong and he seemed youngish, but what mostly struck her was the disagreeable note in his voice.

She tried to escape him, but he'd taken hold of her shoulders and was holding her still while he studied what little he could see of her in the dim light.

"Let me go at once," she said. "I can't stay here."

3

"You can if I say so. You should be at the ball. This part of the house is private. What are you doing here?"

"That is none of your business."

He peered closer. "Good heavens! You're too young for balls. You're little more than a child."

"I am nineteen years old," she said furiously, "I have been presented at court and I've received three proposals of marriage. Which is three more than I wanted, if you must know."

She wished she could see him better, but he had his back to the French windows, and his face was in shadow. But she could sense the grin with which he said,

"What a wealth of experience! So why are you running away like a frightened rabbit?"

She heard footsteps outside, her name being called by Sir Cedric, and groaned.

"Because of that silly creature! I've lost all patience with him."

The next moment the door was pushed open and Sir Cedric rushed into the room.

"There you are," he cried.

"Yes, here I am, but as you see I'm no longer unprotected. Here – "

But to her dismay the strange man had vanished. He must have gone into the garden, she thought. How unchivalrous!

Luckily Sir Cedric was too deep in his emotions to notice her confusion.

"Now I understand," he said. "You never really meant to escape me at all. You fled only to increase my ardour."

"I suppose you think that's why I slapped your face?" she retorted.

"But of course. I was enchanted by your display of

4

maidenly modesty."

Rowena stamped her foot.

"Do stop talking nonsense. And if you come any closer you'll get another 'display of maidenly modesty' that will make your eyes water. And then maybe you'll believe that I mean what I say."

Faced with her bluntness, Sir Cedric tried another approach. With disastrous results.

"Permit me, beloved of my heart, to point out that the world saw us leaving the ballroom in each other's company. Society is censorious. What will they say?"

Rowena gasped, too taken aback by this disgraceful attitude to be able to think of an answer.

Thinking his chance had come he fell to his knees, seized her hands, and began covering them with kisses.

Rowena managed to wrench one hand free but he held the other tightly. She longed to slap him again, but twice in one evening might be unladylike, so she contented herself with bringing her fan down on the top of his head.

By great good luck she managed to strike the place where his hair was thinning. He squealed and released her in order to rub the patch, which stung.

"Go and tell a censorious society about that, if you dare!" she said furiously.

Sir Cedric got to his feet with as much dignity as he could manage, gave her a reproachful look, and made his way slowly out of the room, slamming the door behind him.

Left to herself, Rowena burst into tears of anger and disgust.

"Don't do that," said a voice from the darkness.

She nearly fainted with shock.

"What?"

The strange man stepped out of the shadows. As he

did so, he turned his head just enough to show her a very slight hook in his nose.

"I really admired you up to that point," he said. "Wonderful spirit. Splendid. Don't spoil it by weeping and wailing like any other girl."

"Have you been here all the time?" she demanded in horror.

"Of course. Best entertainment I've ever had."

"Entertainment? He assaulted me, and you just stood there enjoying yourself. You should have come to my aid."

"What for? You didn't need me. I never saw a young lady so well able to take care of herself."

"That is not the point – "

"No, the point – which you'd realise if you stopped to consider it – is that if I'd appeared and knocked him down, as you seem to think I should have done, it would have created a scandal. And that would really have given a censorious society something to relish."

The knowledge that he was right exasperated her. How dare this unmannerly creature get the better of her!

"I'm a stranger to you," he added. "For all you know I might have a dubious reputation, and being found here with me could be enough to ruin you."

"I am not interested in your reputation," she said stiffly.

"Not interested in the reputation of a man whom you're alone with in a dark room? How foolish of you! Did you really leave the ballroom with that buffoon?"

"Yes," she said mortified.

"You should have had more sense. You're a bonny fighter, but you don't know how to behave like a young lady of delicacy. Now be off with you while you're still safe."

"You mean you aren't going to escort me back to the ballroom?"

"And be seen entering with you after such a long absence?" he asked grimly. "No thank you. You may not care for your reputation, but I care for my future. I've no wish to be coerced into marriage. They've tried every trick in the book on me, but that would be one too many."

She gasped with indignation. "Are you daring to suggest that I planned this as a way to marry you? I don't even know who you are."

"I can't decide what to think. Maybe you planned this as a trap, or maybe you are a really silly little girl who thinks she can do as she likes without consequences. Either way, you're not for me."

Rowena's anger almost boiled over. Sensing it, he seized the hand that was holding her fan.

"No, don't use it on me," he said humorously. "Whatever it did to that booby, a display of temper won't have me grovelling at your feet. I've never been at any woman's feet yet, and it certainly won't be yours. Now leave, and return quickly to the ballroom."

She couldn't believe what she was hearing. Had any man ever before behaved in such an ungentlemanly fashion?

Rowena fled.

By the time she had reached the ballroom, she'd calmed down and managed to seem cheerful as she approached her aunt, Lady Pennington.

She had been born plain Susan Thornhill, but had managed to secure Sir Mathew Pennington on the marriage market.

Armed with this lowly title she did her best to help her brother, Colonel Thornhill, find a splendid husband for his daughter and only child, Rowena.

She hosted his lavish parties at their house in Grosvenor Square, and chaperoned Rowena on her frequent invitations.

She worked hard to help her niece but, as Colonel Thornhill was beginning to realise, the wife of a mere knight did not have the entrée to the very highest levels of society.

Also, Sir Mathew was growing peevish at his wife's frequent absences from home. He refused all opportunities to accompany her, preferring a pipe and a good brandy in his own library.

As soon as she entered the ballroom Rowena saw her aunt giving her anxious looks. She smiled in reassurance, but didn't want to talk just then, lest she give something away. So she gave her attention to the young man hurrying towards her.

"I have been looking for you," he said, "I was afraid you had gone home, and forgotten our dance."

"Our dance?" she queried.

"I wrote my name on your card."

"Then let us dance," she said, quickly checking his name on her card, for she could barely recall him. Lord Rennick.

She'd discovered that that was how it was, when you were a successful debutante. Young men came and went in a dream, and it grew hard to tell them apart.

She danced two dances with him, then couples began to drift out onto the balcony to watch some fireworks.

But Lord Rennick clasped her hand and drew her back.

"I have been wanting to get you alone for a long time," he said.

"I think we should join the others," Rowena answered firmly.

"But I want to talk to you – to tell you I love you and I want you to be my wife."

Rowena drew in her breath. Two unwelcome proposals in one evening was more than she could endure.

"Excuse me," she said hurriedly. "My aunt will be looking for me."

She slipped away before he could protest, and found Lady Pennington glad to go home.

*

In his palatial house in Grosvenor Square, Colonel Thornhill was pacing the floor of his library, listening for the sound of carriage wheels that would announce his daughter's return from the ball.

Now and then he glanced at the luxury surrounding him with a kind of dissatisfaction. He was one of the richest men in London, perhaps in the whole country. For years he'd been able to buy whatever he set his heart on.

But now he'd set his heart on something that seemed to be elusive.

A great title for Rowena, and the entrée into high society for himself.

It didn't seem much to ask. Other men bought Earls and Marquises for their daughters, men whose wealth wasn't half of his.

Yet Rowena's first season was passing without a single 'catch'.

Somewhere behind the Colonel a small, elderly man was pottering about the library, occasionally stopping to refill his brandy glass.

This was the Reverend Adrian Farley, his father-in-law. He was a vague, gentle creature who lived with his brash son-in-law solely because he loved his grand-daughter.

The Colonel had taken him in as a duty, but his wife's father made him uneasy. Although now retired, the Reverend Farley was still a man of the cloth. He disapproved of his son-in-law, and often made ironic comments about his ambitions, with what the Colonel thought was a most unclerical relish.

"No sign of her yet," Mr. Farley said now, joining him at the window.

"I don't really expect her so early," said the Colonel. "Not if the ball was a success."

"Rowena is always a success," the old man said, "as far as she can be."

"What the devil do you mean by that?"

"I mean having her chaperoned everywhere by your sister. Got nothing against your sister, mind. Always very civil to me. But if you thought she could sponsor Rowena into high society you were fooling yourself."

"*Lady* Pennington has effected a great many notable introductions – " the Colonel started to say but was stopped by a cackle.

"Lady Pennington is the wife of a knight, no more," Mr. Farley said bluntly. "Couldn't get Rowena presented at court, because she hadn't been presented herself."

"I managed that without her help," the colonel riposted.

"Oh yes, Lady Childen. Tell me, just how many of her son's debts did you have to settle before she agreed?"

"That is beside the point," the Colonel said stiffly.

"Very much to the point if you ask me. Especially as she diddled you. She was supposed to take Rowena to some fancy parties, wasn't she? But the minute the presentation was over she dropped you."

Mr. Farley guffawed. "That must make her the only person ever to pull the wool over your eyes."

"I'm surprised by your interest," the Colonel said frostily, "since you lose no chance to tell me that you think my ambitions for Rowena are absurd."

"They are absurd. And your ambitions aren't for Rowena, but yourself. You want something only that sweet girl can give you, and you make use of her under the guise of doing the best for your daughter."

"That is an outrageous suggestion," said the Colonel through gritted teeth.

"Yes, it is," Mr. Farley observed amiably. "Totally outrageous. But it is also true, and I see it, even if poor little Rowena doesn't."

"Then it amazes me that you should be so concerned at what you see as my sister's deficiencies as a chaperone."

"Not concerned at all," Mr. Farley retorted. "All to the good, if you ask me. Just thought I'd mention that you don't know what you're doing, that's all."

"You lose no occasion to insult me," the Colonel snapped.

"It's not insulting you to say you don't know what you're doing, m'dear fellow. Plain fact. You're not in the army now, you know. No use conducting a marriage market like a military campaign. Although I must admit it gives me a lot of innocent pleasure to watch you bang your head against a brick wall."

"You appear to believe that you have the right to behave as you please in my house. How if I demand that you leave?"

"How if I tell Rowena that you're throwing me out? And why."

This effectively brought the conversation to a standstill. The Colonel knew Rowena was deeply fond of her grandfather and would ask awkward questions about his departure. Nor did he relish the thought of Mr. Farley expressing his opinions too freely to her.

Meeting Mr. Farley's cynical eye, Colonel Thornhill knew he had been checkmated.

For the moment, he promised himself. Only for the moment.

"I need some more brandy," he snapped. "Be good

enough to ring for the footman."

Instead of complying, Mr. Farley brought the brandy decanter himself.

"Load of tomfoolery," he said. "Ring for the footman, when the decanter's standing just a few feet away."

"It is the correct thing to do," the Colonel said between gritted teeth.

"Then the correct thing to do is nonsense," said Mr. Farley, not in the least perturbed. "I wouldn't mind if you kept your nonsense to yourself, but you're spoiling that lovely girl with your daft ideas.

"You used to be a decent fellow, a soldier, solid and upright. Then you made a lot of money and turned soft in the head."

The Colonel pretended not to hear this. Since he couldn't silence Mr. Farley, the only thing to do was become deaf.

To his intense annoyance, he realised that there was much in what his father-in-law said.

He had no illusions about himself. He was a soldier, a rough diamond, who'd made most of his money in America after he'd left the army.

It was a young country, vibrant and full of new ideas. Great things were invented almost every day, and there was money to be made in their development.

As he had grown older and cleverer he had managed to invest in a number of these inventions.

It had been, as Colonel Thornhill had once said, like a volley of guns going off one after another and each one being louder than the last.

Whatever they had discovered or invented in America had made it a nation of rich men. And he had been in the forefront.

He'd stayed in America longer than he'd intended,

building up his fortune, seizing a chance that he knew wouldn't come twice in a lifetime.

Then had come the news that his wife was suffering from an incurable disease. He rushed back to England, arriving too late to see her before she died.

He was a hard man, but he had loved his wife, and his failure to reach her in time was something that still caused him grief.

He had found his daughter Rowena almost a stranger to him. After burying his wife, he sent Rowena to complete her education in a Swiss finishing school, and returned to America.

He only returned when Rowena was eighteen, ready to leave school and become a debutante.

In the last year, she had flowered, and he was astonished when he saw her to realise she had grown into an undoubted beauty.

She was someone, the Colonel thought, every man would stare at and, if he was wise, want to possess.

It was then that he turned his interests and ambitions to his daughter.

He wanted something. And Rowena could give it to him.

Then he began to realise that he had rather neglected her and that if he was to bring his plans to fruition, it would take a lot of careful planning, and cultivating the right people.

Mr. Farley had said the Colonel had gone about it like a military campaign, and up to a point he'd been right.

A campaign needed a base camp, so he bought a magnificent house in Kent which had formerly belonged to an ancient family which went back ten generations, and whose name had been intertwined with the history of England. Not only was the house palatial, but it was surrounded by a vast estate.

Now, he thought proudly, Colonel Thornhill and Miss Rowena Thornhill, were landed gentry. It was a start.

Next she must make her debut in London.

He bought a house in Grosvenor Square, making sure that it was the best and most expensive available. Then he had secured the services of Lady Childen to sponsor Rowena's presentation at court.

It had cost him a fabulous sum, but he didn't mind if he got what he wanted.

But he hadn't. After the presentation Lady Childen had refused to help any further. As Mr. Farley had vulgarly said, she'd 'diddled him'.

Rowena moved in society, but she had no title. She had no connections. She lacked the shared background of the aristocrats. Gradually the Colonel realised that there was something lacking in his plan of action.

He found that he could fill his house with all manner of guests – of a certain type. City men and the lower rungs of the aristocracy.

But these weren't the prey he was after. It was the Dukes, Earls, Marquises that he wanted. And their doors remained mostly closed to him.

The only place he could meet the higher ranks was at the Clipper Club, one of the best clubs in London. Its members owned sea-going vessels of all kinds, and the chief founder had owned a large clipper ship. Hence the name.

Even the Prince of Wales, an enthusiastic sailor, had been seen in their palatial establishment in Piccadilly. He wasn't a member, but he often appeared as a guest.

The members gave themselves airs and boasted that only the best was allowed to join. But the Colonel knew how much in debt each man was, how much they had paid for their gorgeous ships, and whether they could really afford it.

He bought up their debts, and when he presented himself for membership nobody dared to blackball him.

Now he met the crème de la crème of British aristocracy, and invited them to his house. Although some refused, many came, intrigued by the stories they'd heard of his enormous wealth.

They drank his brandy and smoked his cigars. Many of them sighed after his daughter's beauty. But they thought twice before offering marriage to a girl without a background.

That was the blunt truth of the matter, and the more the Colonel thought of it, the more he realised that he needed another strategy, one that would bring him everything he wanted.

CHAPTER TWO

At last the Colonel heard the sound of carriage wheels, and in a few moments his daughter had arrived home with her aunt.

Mr. Farley greeted his beloved grand-daughter affectionately, while the Colonel drew his sister aside for a report on the evening.

"I gather Rowena received a declaration tonight," Lady Pennington told him quietly. "And refused it absolutely."

"Without consulting me?" the Colonel demanded.

"Well, it was only Sir Cedric Humboldt. Scarcely a great catch. Rowena seems to have been rather annoyed with him."

The Colonel frowned. Certainly Sir Cedric wasn't the kind of title he wanted for his daughter, yet Rowena's independent spirit disturbed him. It would be as well to warn her of her duty, lest she throw away her chances.

So when his sister had departed and Mr. Farley had been persuaded to go to bed, he broached the subject.

"I would have preferred that you refer your suitor to me, before refusing him," he said, speaking kindly but firmly.

"But why Papa? I wouldn't dream of marrying such a silly man."

"I hope you weren't impolite to him. Tell me exactly what happened."

Rowena gave him only a very rough description of the scene, leaving out the fact that Sir Cedric had gone down on his knees, and that she had used her fan on him. Nor did she mention the strange man who had spoken to her so rudely. The memory still filled her with mortification.

When she had finished her father was silent awhile before saying,

"It has been a great wish of mine, for a long time, that you should make a fine marriage. I want you to be on the top of the social world and not, as we are at the moment, at the bottom."

Rowena stared at him. "Why are we on the bottom?" she asked innocently.

"Because my dear, we are of no particular importance except that I am a rich man. But if I could see you a part of the English aristocracy, married to a Duke or an Earl – "

Rowena stared at him. Then she laughed.

"Oh, Papa, you cannot expect me to do that!"

"Why not?" he demanded. "Behind their fine facades, the aristocracy is often deep in debt. Keeping up an ancestral home takes money, and most of them only know how to spend money, not make it."

"And you know how to make it, Papa," Rowena said, nodding. "Everyone says you are a brilliant man and I realise they are referring to the fortune you made abroad.

"But dear Papa, you cannot expect every Englishman to succeed as you have. Of course I know that when they propose to me, they are also proposing to your money."

"Of course," the Colonel answered sharply. "Money! Money! That is all most men want. Well and good if it makes them play into my hands. If I have to buy my son-in-law, then I will aim for the best."

"But I don't want you to buy me a husband, Papa," she protested.

"It will have nothing to do with you. I know what's best for you, and you must trust me in this."

Rowena stared at him, slightly shocked. She had been treating the subject lightly, almost as a joke. Now she began to see that perhaps her father saw her as a commodity in a commercial transaction. His money for a great title.

She tried to push the thought away. It was surely impossible. But it left a shadow of unease and she soon made an excuse to go to bed.

Once in her own room she sat down in front of the mirror and stared at herself as if she had never seen her reflection before.

She would be very stupid if she had not known she was pretty. That her fair hair had touches of gold in it. Her eyes were very blue. In fact, she was what people called, 'an English beauty'. It was something she had been teased about at school.

Now as she looked at herself knowing without being conceited that she was lovely, she sensed, almost as if someone was saying it to her, that the men who were asking her to be their wife did not love her, but her father's money.

"Money! Money! Money!" she said to herself. "That is what they are seeking and that is what they think they have found in me. And Papa knew about this all the time."

She had always realised that her reputation as an heiress was one of her attractions, but it had never before occurred to her that her father might actually be plotting to make use of other men's weaknesses, scheming to sell his daughter to the man who could offer the greatest worldly advantage.

But tonight he had lifted the edge of a curtain and revealed an ugly truth.

He had a plan in place. Just as he had wanted an ancient house and estate, with its history going back for many years, he also wanted a son-in-law about whom he could say the same.

Then she recalled that rude man saying,

'I've no wish to be coerced into marriage. They've tried every trick in the book on me, but that would be one too many.'

It seemed that he too was being pursued for reasons that had nothing to do with love.

Was this, then, the truth about the marriage game as society played it? Was there nothing else but scheming for advantage?

'But I have no intention of making such a marriage,' Rowena told herself. 'I'll marry a man I love, or I won't marry at all.'

With her maid's help she undressed quickly and got into bed, where she lay in the darkness, a prey to troubled thoughts.

Why had she not told her aunt or her father about the strange man at the ball? It was almost as though he'd cast a spell which had kept her silent.

He'd been impolite, unflattering. In fact he'd behaved as no man of her acquaintance had behaved before, as though he cared for nobody's opinion. He would do and say precisely what he wished, and if people disapproved, he would defy them.

Every rule of delicacy she'd been taught told her that this was shockingly improper. Yet during those few minutes in his company, she had known a sense of electric excitement she'd never felt before.

It was as though all the bells in the world had started ringing together. And she had responded to those wild vibrations, whether she wanted to or not.

It was a disturbing memory. But in all likelihood she would never meet him again.

After a while she heard a knock on the door, and knew that her father wanted to speak to her. But she didn't want to talk to him until she had thought some more about what he'd said. So she pretended to be asleep, and after a while he went away.

She lay awake staring into the darkness, wondering what the misty future held.

'Perhaps I am wicked to defy Papa,' she thought. 'If I was a sensible, well-behaved daughter I would do as he wished and marry a title without asking for more.'

Then as if she was controlled not by her own thoughts, but those which came from another world, she sat up in bed.

'No, I am not being wicked!' she told herself. 'I want only what every woman wants, and has the right to fight for – love, the real love which comes from the heart and when she finds the right man, she feels the same for him as he feels for her.

'That is what I will seek. Not social grandeur but love, love, love.'

She jumped out of bed and went to the window. She wanted to shout the words through the windows to the flowers. Then she told herself she must behave discreetly. If she was to save herself from being sacrificed on the altar of social ambition, she must be subtle.

But she knew however much she raged, however much she tried to remain herself, she would inevitably be pushed, pleaded, begged and ordered to marry the man her father had chosen for her.

'What am I to do? Oh God, what am I to do?' Rowena asked herself.

But the only answer was the soft breeze in the trees, and the moon peering at her through the branches.

Colonel Thornhill had certainly chosen his house well. Haverwick Castle was in Kent, not too far from Dover, where his new ship, *The Adventurer*, was moored.

When he decided to move to Kent at the end of the season, it was as though a tidal wave had been set in motion. Colonel Thornhill and his family travelled in a state that the highest nobility in the land might have envied.

The servants and the luggage travelled a day earlier, in order to prepare the house for their master's arrival. They left behind only a skeleton staff to minister to the family on the last day.

The following morning the Colonel, Miss Thornhill, and Mr. Farley, climbed aboard the Colonel's grandiose carriage. Two footmen climbed up behind, the coachman sat on the box, and they were ready to be conveyed to the railway station, to take the train to Dover.

Behind them came a much smaller carriage with no footmen. It contained the Colonel's valet, his secretary, Rowena's lofty dresser, and Jenny, the maid who fetched and carried for the dresser.

When everyone was ready the little procession departed in state for the railway station.

There they embarked on a train for Dover, where they were met by a landau, a four seater open carriage, drawn by a team of four matching horses. In this elegant equipage they covered the few miles to their country home.

They arrived to find Haverwick Castle in perfect condition, because the servants had been working night and day to get it in order. Now they all lined up to greet their employers.

Despite its name it wasn't a real castle but a huge, magnificent house, made of beautiful grey stone. The Colonel had bought everything the departing family had to sell, not just the house but the furniture, ornaments, pictures.

There were some fine old masters on the walls, but there were also family portraits of ancestors in silks and ruffles, farthingales, doublet and hose.

Anyone who didn't know the truth might have believed that these were Thornhill ancestors.

When Rowena had first seen them she'd thought them rather fun. But now she understood that her father was trying to seem something that he was not, and it made her uneasy.

"And he wants me too to pretend to be something that I'm not," she said to her grandfather. "And I can't do it."

"I know my dear," said the old man sympathetically. "I wish he'd give up this idea. He wasn't always so hard and ambitious, but now he thinks of nothing but grandeur."

They were enjoying a few days alone together while the Colonel went to Dover to make arrangements for *The Adventurer's* sea trials. Rowena loved her grandfather, who was the only man she knew really well.

Until her father returned home the year before, she had lived with Mama and Grandpapa. Mama had been in ill health and she had been much thrown into her grandfather's company. The old man, and the young girl had soon become good friends and staunch champions of each other.

They had wept together when Mama died, while Colonel Thornhill was still on the high seas, in a vain attempt to reach home in time. By the time he arrived their tears had dried, and he had seemed almost a stranger.

Now it was a delight to be alone for a while, and talk about the old times when her mother had been alive. Her mind went back to the very early days when Mama had taught her to pray, with Grandpapa's help.

"I always knew my prayers would be heard," she said now as they strolled together in the garden, but I never really thought they could influence or alter my life."

"Whatever did you imagine God did with your prayers, my love," Mr. Farley teased her kindly. "Hide them away and forget them?"

"No, but I know how very busy he must be – "

"He is, my dear," the clergyman said. "But you must trust him to answer your prayers in his own way. He won't send down a thunderbolt from heaven. The answer will come unexpectedly, and at first you might not even recognise it."

"Oh but I will," Rowena said fervently. "The answer must be the man I love, and when I meet him I'll know him at once."

Mr. Farley merely smiled and looked at her fondly.

Surprisingly, even to herself, Rowena did not miss the glamour or the thrill of being the debutante of the year. She had always loved the country, and now she had the added delight of fine horses to ride, for her father had filled his stables with splendid beasts.

Near to the stables, there was a flat piece of land where he had ordered jumps to be built. Rowena found it thrilling to take her horse over them one by one.

Although at first she was rather afraid of falling, she soon learnt to jump as well as she could ride and enjoyed every moment of it.

The only thing to spoil her pleasure was that she couldn't go as fast as she would like. Burdit, her groom was a severe person, always reminding her of what 'the Colonel said.' And Mr. Farley was a nervous rider, who couldn't share her desire to gallop.

"Oh Grandpapa," she said one afternoon, "don't you just long to throw off restraint and fly like the wind."

"No my dear, I don't. I'm much too old. And why should you want to do something that might be dangerous?

Suppose you fell and got mud on that beautiful habit?"

Rowena laughed, for she knew she looked her best in a brand new riding habit of deep blue velvet, with lace ruffles at the throat, held by a pearl pin.

She was mounted on Ella, a dainty, spirited little black mare, which was her favorite mount, and the two of them would have turned any man's head.

"I promise not to muddy my habit, Grandpapa," she said mischievously.

"Well, you do as you want. You're young, and youth is the time for flying." He winked. "Don't worry. I won't tell on you to your Papa."

"It's not Papa I worry about. I'm much more afraid of Burdit."

He put a finger over his lips. Rowena chuckled and galloped away, feeling Ella gather speed beneath her. They seemed to understand each other by instinct.

It was wonderful to be going really fast, feeling the wind whistle past her head. Faster and faster she went, deep into the countryside, rejoicing in her freedom, knowing that it couldn't last.

'I could keep on like this,' she thought, 'just galloping forever, leaving the problems behind me.'

She knew she couldn't really do such a thing, but it was such a delightful dream that she indulged it for a moment, and in that moment she made the fatal mistake of taking her mind off what she was doing.

Then she saw it, a fallen tree trunk straight ahead in her path. It was too late to think, too late for anything except to gather herself together, encourage Ella to leap high and far, and pray that there would be nothing on the other side.

She was lucky. She landed safely. But almost at once she realised that she was not alone. A man on horseback was galloping towards her and she had landed straight into his path.

He halted sharply. Taken by surprise his horse reared and plunged. He was a huge beast, and his great hooves seemed to tower over the delicate Ella, frightening her, so that she too began to rear.

Rowena fought to stay in the saddle but Ella was maddened with alarm and out of control. She kicked and plunged, while Rowena clung on and prayed not to be thrown.

With an oath the man jumped down to the ground and dashed for Ella's head. He didn't seem afraid of her flying hooves, but dodged them easily, seizing the bridle, and forcing the mare to be still.

"Thank you so much," Rowena gasped.

'He must be a servant,' she thought. 'He was wearing buckskin breeches and a white shirt, with no jacket over it. No gentleman would dress so informally.'

Yet when he spoke his voice was cultured and his manner had authority.

"Get down," he said curtly.

"I – what did you say?"

"I said get down. I have things to say to you and I don't want to say them looking up."

Suddenly she grew still. There was something horribly familiar about the set of his head, and even more horribly familiar about his voice. Then a slight turn of his head showed her the faint hook in his nose.

"You," she breathed. "*You*!"

"Yes," he said. "We have met before. Now get down."

"I would rather – "

He didn't let her finish but reached up to settle his hands about her waist.

"How dare you!" she flashed. "Let me go at once. *Did you hear me?*"

The last words were almost a shriek as, ignoring her orders, he raised her in the air and lowered her to the ground, releasing her waist but keeping hold of one wrist.

"How dare you touch me!" she said furiously. "You are no gentleman!"

He gave a sardonic grin. "Coming from a girl who doesn't know how to behave like a lady, that accusation fails to move me."

"You have no right to say such a thing!"

"At the ball you went wandering away from your chaperone and very nearly paid a heavy price for it. Today you go galloping about the country without a groom."

Now she saw him more clearly, she realised that this man was no servant. He had a lean face with fine features, a high, noble forehead and very dark eyes.

His hair too was dark, almost black. His mouth was wide and mobile, his chin firm.

He behaved like a man used to giving orders and having them obeyed instantly. Rowena felt a moment's pity for anyone who defied him, then instantly decided to do so.

The more he tried to bully her, the more she would refuse to be bullied. He would see that he was dealing with Miss Thornhill of Haverwick Castle.

"You're making a great mistake in treating me like this. Do you know who I am?"

"No, you silly child, and I don't want to. Don't you realise that nothing could turn this into a scandal more certainly than your name being bandied around – even from your own lips? What are you thinking of to ride out alone?"

"That does not concern you," she said trying to wrench free from him.

But he refused to release her wrist. His grip was light

but implacable.

"I'm making it my concern, since you keep popping up before me. I warned you last time, if you're trying to trap a husband this is no way to go about it."

"Me?" she echoed, hardly able to believe her ears. "Me, trap a husband? I can assure you sir, nothing is further from my mind."

"I hope you're telling the truth. Nothing puts a man off more than a girl who appears desperate."

She was almost beyond speech. To be called desperate! She, who was used to being pursued by men, and rejecting then! She managed to find voice enough to say,

"You have a short memory sir, if you think I'm at my last prayers. Have you forgotten that at our first meeting, I was rejecting a man who was pursuing me?"

"That fool? I should think so indeed. You should be after much bigger fish."

"*I am not fishing!*"

"Nonsense! A girl of your age is always fishing. It's her business to get married."

"Always assuming she can find a man who's tolerable," Rowena snapped. "In my experience, most of them aren't. And the conceited ones are the worst. Men who imagine every woman is after them are the most impossible bores."

His eyes narrowed. "Very clever, madam."

"You obviously recognise yourself in the description" Rowena continued. "Conceited, boorish, ill-bred – "

"You're wasting your time," he said impatiently. "I'm as impervious to insults as to flattery. Forget about me."

"That is a little difficult when you keep haunting me."

"I would rather have said it is *you* haunting *me*. Suppose it hadn't been me, but some ruffian intent on harming you – "

"As far as I'm concerned, you are a ruffian."

"If you think that, you little goose, you've plainly never encountered one" he retorted. "A real desperado would have stolen that pretty pearl by now. He might even be tempted to steal more."

"I – I don't know what you mean."

"I think you do." Putting his fingers beneath her chin he tipped it up so that he met her deep blue eyes, full of anger. She tried to pull away but he slipped his arm about her first, drawing her closer, so that she could feel the warmth of his hard body against hers.

"I think you know just how lovely you are, how vividly the blue of your eyes gleams, how softly your skin glows. And I'm quite sure you know that your lips are so temptingly curved that no man could possibly resist them."

He gave a slow smile, like a man relishing the prospect before him.

"Perhaps I won't even try to resist," he mused. "Your mouth was made for kisses, so why shouldn't I steal one?"

"Because it wouldn't be the act of a gentleman," she gasped.

"But I'm not a gentleman. I'm an evil doer, lying in wait for you, and now I've got you at my mercy. Entirely your own fault. You really should be more careful, madam."

Rowena's heart was thumping wildly, though whether with rage or something else, she couldn't have said. She only knew that she was filled with strange sensations that she had never known before. She didn't know whether she liked them, but they were thrilling.

She thought there was something almost devilish about him. In the same moment it struck her forcefully that he was the most handsome man she had ever seen. The thought was shocking.

How could a man be so attractive and so wicked?

"Nothing to say?" he asked.

"I have this to say. If you dare to kiss me, I will make you pay a heavy price for it even if it takes me all my days.

"Beware, sir. You think because I'm a helpless girl you can do as you like with me. You will find differently. You have been warned."

Into his eyes came a reluctant admiration, and his gaze softened.

"You're wrong, madam, I don't think you're helpless. Any woman who can defy me at this moment has resources of brains and courage that I have to respect."

Her unyielding gaze was still on him.

"I am not moved by flattery," she said firmly. "And I demand that you release me at once."

He gave a grin that made him even more blazingly attractive than ever, while strangely emphasising his hint of the devilish.

"I've met so few women who weren't moved by flattery," he mused.

"Then you've finally met your match," she riposted. "And when I say 'met your match' that is not a suggestion of marriage. You are, in fact, the last man on earth I would stoop to marry.

"You could be the richest man in the world and brother to the Prince of Wales, and I would still say you are a conceited, boorish, mannerless creature who doesn't know how to behave like a gentleman.

"I pity the woman who is finally so unfortunate as to take your name. And if ever I hear who she is, I shall send her my condolences."

His grin broadened until he burst out laughing.

"Capital! If I had a glass I would drink to your spirit.

But how will you sympathise with my bride when you don't know my name?"

"I'll hear of it soon enough. A creature like yourself couldn't be at large for long without all society knowing. Now let me go."

This time he did so.

"I feel tolerably sure that I shall hear of you too, madam. Such an unusual young woman must surely create her own disturbance wherever she goes. I'll assist you to mount."

If she could have mounted without him she would have done so, but as she had no choice she accepted his help with dignity.

Ella had been contentedly munching grass while they fought. Now she remained steady while the man placed his hands about her waist and tossed her up into the saddle as though she weighed nothing.

She had a feeling of blazing awareness as long as his hands were around her waist. Then he held up his whip in a gesture of salute.

"Here's to our next meeting."

"Here's to never meeting again," she riposted lightly.

The next moment she'd wheeled away, urged Ella into a gallop and soared back over the fallen tree trunk.

She found Mr. Farley still waiting in the same spot. He'd dismounted and was sitting on a tree stump, enjoying a cigar.

"There you are, my darling," he cried in delight. "Did you enjoy your ride?"

"It was very interesting," she said crisply. "Do let us go home quickly, Grandpapa. Burdit will be in such a fret."

CHAPTER THREE

They reached the house to be met with the news that Colonel Thornhill had returned from Dover. Rowena ran to greet him.

"Oh Papa, how well you look! Did you have a good time?"

"Excellent, my darling."

"Did *The Adventurer* go well? Oh, I'm longing to see her."

"And so you shall. I plan to return tomorrow to take her for sea trials, and I thought you would like to go with me."

"Papa!" she cried in delight. "That will be wonderful. Can Grandpapa come with us? He loves the sea so much."

"No, thank you, my dear," Mr. Farley said from the doorway, where he'd heard everything. "I fancy a few restful days here."

When Rowena had slipped away to change the Colonel said abruptly, "Thank you!"

"The best thing for you and Rowena is to have a few days in each other's company, away from society. This is your chance, and I wouldn't want to be in the way."

"I'm grateful." The Colonel grinned suddenly, becoming a much nicer man. "But I must be honest with you. We shan't be entirely free from society. The Prince of

Wales will be in Dover, trying out his new yacht."

"Well, I don't suppose you're trying to marry Rowena off to him!"

Both men laughed, and finished the day in perfect accord. At supper that night Rowena thought she'd never spent such a pleasant time.

Again, she did not mention the mysterious stranger to her father. But in the pleasure of going to sea she was almost able to forget him.

Almost.

But not quite.

*

The next morning the landau was waiting at the door to convey them the few miles to Dover. There they were to stay at the Ship Hotel, to save a journey home every evening, and, as before, servants had gone ahead to ensure that everything was up to their employer's standards.

"But I don't quite see why I had to take my dresser as well," Rowena observed when they were moving. "She hates the sea, and surely Jenny would have been enough to attend me on board?"

"But we shan't be on board all the time," her father told her. "I've saved this as a surprise. The Prince of Wales will be in Dover this week, and I have every hope that we will meet him."

"The Prince of Wales," she breathed. "How wonderful! Will Princess Alexandra be with him?"

The Colonel coughed awkwardly. "No, my dear. Her Royal Highness remains at home with their children."

He didn't feel equal to explaining to his innocent daughter that the Prince was a notoriously unfaithful husband, who left his wife behind whenever possible.

Their rooms were ready at the Ship Hotel, and after

changing her clothes Rowena was ready and eager to explore *The Adventurer*, which she had never seen before.

As soon as she saw it Rowena realised that she had been somewhat misled by the term 'yacht'. This was actually a steamship, one hundred and fifty feet long, and containing, according to her father, 'every modern luxury'.

She had to agree with him when she inspected the cabins and he showed her the cunning arrangement for keeping everyone cool.

"When the ship's in motion the working of the paddles causes fresh air to circulate by means of fans worked by the steam engines, so that the air of the whole ship is changed in half an hour."

"That sounds very agreeable," she said. "And I like the awning on the upper deck too. It'll be so pleasant to be protected from the sun in hot weather."

Down below there was even more to make her stare. Apart from the spacious saloon, dining room and kitchens, there were ten double cabins, each with two sleeping berths, a sofa and elegant fittings.

In the stern of the ship was a smoking room, with a small billiard table.

As well as the kitchens being well stocked, there was a fine wine cellar, and the ship's tanks could hold two thousand gallons of water. Nothing was lacking for a comfortable journey.

"Why Papa," she said, amazed, "it's like a whole little world. You could hold a country house party here."

"That's just what I thought," he said. "And it's exactly what I mean to do. What could be nicer than a few days cruising in such comfort?"

That night he gave a party. Several aristocratic members of the Clipper Club were there, some with wives and daughters, and for once their rank made no difference.

They all had titles of some kind, and the Thornhills had none, yet the atmosphere was charmingly informal, for here they were all sailors together. Or so they enjoyed telling themselves.

"I say, did you hear that Wenfield is in Dover now?" Lord Stanton said languidly. "They say he's disposed of the *Ariadne*."

"No choice after all the debts he inherited," another man said. "Pity. I believe he enjoyed the sea."

"Anyone know who bought it?" Lord Stanton asked.

"Someone the Prince introduced to him. He and Wenfield are thick as thieves."

"Who's Wenfield?" Rowena asked Jane Stanton who was standing close to her father.

"The Duke of Wenfield. He came into the title last year, rather unexpectedly. It should have gone to his cousin, but he died after a fall in the hunting field, so when the old Duke died it went to Mark."

"Do you know him?"

"I've met him twice and danced with him once. He's rather grim and serious, which is all very well in its way, but I like a man who'll play the society game without being disagreeable about it."

"What do you call the society game?"

"Pretty compliments, making you feel that you're a goddess, nothing is too good for you. No girl ever got a pretty compliment from Mark."

"But why should he pay compliments that aren't sincere?" Rowena asked. "Perhaps he's just an honest man."

"But who wants a man who's honest in the ballroom?" Jane asked. "My Frank says the most delightful things to me, hour after hour."

The Honourable Francis Dillon was the man she would marry in a few months. Rowena considered him an amiable nonentity, harmless and rather dull. But Jane thought he was perfect in every way, so Rowena smiled and said something kind about him.

She realised that Jane had found exactly what she herself wanted. She was betrothed to a man she adored and who adored her, yet Rowena couldn't envy her friend.

'I should hope for a man with more brains than poor Frank,' she thought. 'Oh dear, I'm afraid I'm becoming rather demanding. But somewhere in the world there must surely be a man I can love and also respect. Is that really asking for the moon?'

Thinking of some of the men of her acquaintance, she began to fear that it was.

Next day they took the boat out and had a splendid day on the waves. Rowena instinctively loved the sea, and when they returned she felt more in sympathy with her father than she had done ever since she had discovered his plan for her.

As they drifted home in the evening she leaned over the rail, gazing across the sea, wondering what the future held for her.

"I wish we could sail on like this forever," she told her father, who came to stand beside her. "And just forget about worldly ambition."

"You know I only want the very best for you, don't you Rowena darling?" he said. "I want you to be as happy as I was with your mother. We loved each other from the first moment."

"But you left Mama and went off to America," Rowena said quietly.

"I did that because I wanted her to have anything she wanted, however expensive it might be."

"But she didn't want things, she wanted to be with you," Rowena protested. "She missed you so much."

Her father hesitated for a moment before he said: "I

will never forgive myself for not being with her when she died. I hurried home, but I arrived too late."

Rowena knew by the pain in his voice he was speaking the truth. She slipped her arm into his.

"I know you loved her, Papa," she said. "That kind of love is what I want too, some day. But I haven't found it so far."

"Are you quite sure of that?" her father asked.

"Quite, quite sure," she replied.

"Then we must just go on looking. After all I cannot live for ever and I would hate you to be alone in that great house without a man to look after you."

"You are only trying to make me feel sorry for you," Rowena retorted, attempting to make him smile. "You are in very good health and are likely to live for at least another forty or fifty years."

Her father held up his hands. "Heaven forbid!" he exclaimed.

"Nonsense," Rowena said. "You will enjoy every moment of it and I will do my best to please you. But I won't marry a man who is only interested in your money and not in me."

"I think you could make any man happy, but I would still like you to have a coronet on your head."

Rowena laughed and kissed him.

But when she went to bed that night she was thinking that sooner or later she would have to find a husband.

Her father would never be content until he was certain the great fortune he had acquired would be looked after by a sensible man, with a great name.

This happy time together couldn't last. She sensed the battle was about to begin, and she was right.

The following day they received an invitation from

Lord Stanton to a 'small reception' he was giving aboard his boat to meet 'a very distinguished guest'.

"Papa," Rowena said, awed, "is this – ?"

"Hush my dear. Just be quite certain that you are looking your very best."

It soon became clear exactly what that meant. Mrs. Kilton, her dresser, had with her a lavish evening dress of ivory satin, heavily trimmed with lace. The waist was tiny, the bustle impressive. It was the very latest Paris fashion and had arrived too late for Rowena to wear it during the season.

The front was very low, almost immodestly low, she thought as Mrs. Kilton fastened it at the back.

"You'll understand why in a minute," Mrs. Kilton said.

Under Rowena's astonished eyes she opened a large jewel box and took out a three stranded pearl necklace, which she draped about Rowena's neck. Then she fitted a pearl tiara on her shining golden hair, heavy pearl drops went on her ears. And to finish there was a splendid five stranded pearl bracelet.

Rowena gasped at her own magnificence. The mirror reflected back a very fine lady indeed, but it didn't look at all like her.

"Surely I recognise these pearls," she said. "I've seen them in one of the portraits at Haverwick Castle."

"Indeed you have, miss. They're the family pearls of the Haverwick family. Your Papa had them specially cleaned to be ready for you."

So the family had had to sell their jewels as well as everything else, she thought. It made her feel uneasy to be so grand at the expense of somebody else's misfortune.

She said as much to her father when he came to collect her.

"But of course you must look fine, my dear. Anything less would be an insult to His Royal Highness."

Rowena had met the Prince once before. Since the death of Albert, the Prince Consort, Queen Victoria had gone into seclusion, and debutantes were presented to the Prince and Princess of Wales. But it had all been over in a moment, and she was curious to meet him again at a smaller gathering.

The carriage conveyed them to where Lord Stanton's ship was berthed. Rowena saw her father glancing over it and knew he was thinking that it wasn't as splendid as his own. But then, he lacked the standing to invite the Prince to his yacht.

Nonetheless, when they entered the great saloon below, the Prince of Wales greeted him very affably as a fellow member of the Clipper Club.

"Thornhill, m'dear chap. Glad to see you."

The Prince was in his middle thirties with a fleshy face, whose petulance was hidden beneath a beard. He was married with four children, and lived the life of a bachelor, doing as he pleased, surrounded by loyal friends to minister to his every whim. Whether it was drinking heavily, gambling, disporting himself with willing ladies, he could always be sure that his dissipations would be hidden from the world and, if possible, from his wife.

Yet he had a great deal of charm that won him forgiveness wherever he went. Within a few minutes of his turning his attention onto her, Rowena felt that he must be the most delightful man alive.

"Only my very dearest friends are here tonight," he assured her. "Some, of course, don't know each other, so then it's my pleasure to introduce them. But perhaps you've already met the Duke of Wenfield?"

Rowena assured him that she hadn't. She didn't add that since speaking to Jane, she was fascinated by the sound of the man who 'wouldn't play society's game'.

"And you the debutante of the year?" he teased her.

"Certainly you must meet Mark, for nobody is more of a connoisseur of beauty – unless perhaps myself." He winked at her, then called, "Mark, come and meet Miss Rowena Thornhill."

Rowena looked up smiling at the coldly handsome man who came forward. Then her smile faded and her heart began to thump.

This was her evil genius, the man who appeared out of nowhere and was frank about his poor opinion of her. This was the last man in the world she wanted to meet.

"Miss Thornhill," said His Royal Highness, "allow me to present my good friend, Mark, Duke of Wenfield. Mark, Colonel Thornhill, and his daughter Rowena."

"Sir." Rowena inclined her head as she spoke, and received in return a murmured, "enchanted," as the Duke carried her hand to his lips.

Looking him in the eye, she realised that her first shocked impression hadn't been a mistake. This really was the man she'd met at the ball, and who'd hauled her down from her horse so ungraciously.

At their first meeting she'd seen him only in semi-darkness, and had received no more than an impression of force and authority. Plus she was sure that he'd been plainly dressed, and not attired in ballroom finery. When they'd met on horseback he'd been clad in a white shirt and plain breeches, with nothing to suggest his grand title.

He had seized her ungently, and held her improperly close, so that she'd had a clear view of his face with its fine features. If she hadn't been angry with him she would have called it a sensitive face, even handsome, with its dark, expressive eyes and firm mouth. But because she'd been in a rage, she'd noticed only the stubbornness of his chin.

She couldn't determine his age. His face was that of a young man, but there was a hint of grey at his temples, and maturity in his manner. Certainly he wasn't a callow boy like too many of the young men she met.

He was finely dressed, as befitted a friend of the Prince of Wales, in white tie and tails, which he wore with an unmistakable air. Now there was no doubt that this man was an aristocrat, a man of pride, even of arrogance. Rowena felt that he had taken unfair advantage of her in concealing this in their previous meetings.

But perhaps he wouldn't remember her, or would pretend not to. That, she felt, would be the gentlemanly thing for him to do.

Behind them were more guests awaiting an introduction to the Prince, making it necessary for them to move away.

"A very fine boat, you have," the Duke remarked to Colonel Thornhill. "She was pointed out to me."

"I hope you will feel free to come and look her over whenever you wish," the Colonel said at once.

"Thank you. I shall avail myself of your invitation. And you, Miss Thornhill, are you fond of the sea?"

"I haven't been to sea very much, but I have enjoyed what little I've seen," she said, managing to speak with composure.

"Does *The Adventurer* live up to her reputation?"

"I do not know, sir, what her reputation may be – "

"As the finest ship in port."

"In any case, I beg you not to appeal to me for an opinion. I am ignorant of such matters."

The cool tone in which she spoke amounted almost to a rebuff. Certainly, she thought, nobody could accuse her of trying to lure this man on.

"You are too modest, I am sure," he said graciously.

"No, why should you be sure of any such thing? You

know nothing about me."

"Rowena, my dear!" her father protested with a frown. "You must forgive my daughter, sir. She is sometimes a little too free-spoken."

"But I like that," the Duke replied. "So much better than the simpering one endures from too many young females. How refreshing to meet a woman who speaks her mind."

"You are too kind to say so," the Colonel replied.

So that was it, Rowena thought. The Duke of Wenfield was the quarry her father had in his sights. And the Duke undoubtedly knew it. He was used to being pursued, he'd told her as much. And doubtless he despised her father for his tactics.

How dare he! she thought. It was one thing for her to deprecate Papa's eagerness to marry her off well. But for this proud man to think badly of them both was quite another matter. She wouldn't allow it.

Putting her head up she adopted a teasing manner.

"Really, Papa, the Duke isn't kind at all. He merely respects my right to my own thoughts. I don't need his permission to think – or say – whatever I please. Do I, sir?"

She swung round on the Duke suddenly, a pretty, coaxing smile on her face. Only he could see that above that smile her eyes were full of cool challenge.

"Indeed you do not," he responded at once. "May I say that any man who tried to deny Miss Thornhill her liberty of speech and thought would be churlish indeed?"

There was an equal challenge in his own eyes, and a glimmer of amusement.

The Colonel began to repeat, "You are too kind – " then stopped. He was not a sensitive man, or even, socially, a very clever one. But he'd managed to discern that this conversation was moving into uncharted waters.

"Thornhill, do you play cards?" That was the Prince calling.

The Colonel bowed and departed, not without a certain relief.

"It's rather stuffy in here," the Duke said. "Shall we take a turn about the deck, Miss Thornhill?"

He held out his arm to her, and she took it. Together they turned to face the Prince, so that the Duke could bow, and she could curtsey, silently seeking permission to leave the royal presence. It was granted with a nod, and they retired from the saloon, watched by many curious eyes.

The weather was warm and it was very pleasant on deck. Above them a brilliant moon floated in a sea of stars. For a while they walked together in silence, her arm through his, while she tried to think of something to say, and failed.

"So now we both know the answer to our questions, Miss Thornhill," the Duke said at last.

"Our questions?"

"Surely you're not going to be missish and pretend not to understand me? We have each wondered about the other's identity, and now we know."

"I think the least said about that matter the better," Rowena replied with an attempt at dignity. "We both said things we regret – "

"I didn't. I regret nothing that I said or did."

"Then – " she checked herself.

"Surely, Miss Thornhill, you're not going to tell me that I'm not a gentleman?" There was no mistaking the irony in his voice. "I thought we'd settled that."

"No, we've settled that you're a Duke," Rowena said. "A gentleman is quite another matter."

"Oh, well done, Miss Thornhill. *Touché!* I laid myself wide open for that, didn't I?"

Rowena took a deep breath. This man's self confidence was insufferable. Was there nothing she could say to disconcert him?

"Yes, I think you did," she replied. "I have no reason to think well of you, and I see no point in continuing this conversation."

"I see every point. Chiefly the fact that if we end it too soon, your father will be deeply disappointed. So, for that matter, will the Prince."

"It can be of no possible interest to the Prince."

"Come, don't be naïve. The Prince is always loyal to his friends. He vowed to introduce me to a great heiress."

"Indeed!" she replied in a freezing voice.

"I told him that I had no interest in heiresses, and that he shouldn't trouble himself, but when he gets an idea in his head there's no stopping him. This is the result."

"And no doubt the Prince is expecting an interesting announcement," Rowena said bitterly. "As is my father. Well, Duke, I suggest we return now and tell them plainly to put the idea out of their minds, as we dislike each other too much to contemplate it."

"But do we dislike each other?" he mused.

"Yes," she said firmly. "We do. We shall also add that we would be quite happy never to see each other again."

"I don't think that would be wise."

"I don't care if it's wise or not. It is what I wish to do."

"It would earn the Prince's displeasure and your social ruin."

"At this precise moment my social ruin is the last thing that concerns me. In fact it would be preferable to the kind of unpleasant experiences my father subjects me to in the name of his ambition."

"You are very frank, madam. Most ladies, let me tell

43

you, do not find my attentions an unpleasant experience."

"I am sure of it. You have already boasted how anxious they all were to trap you into marriage. You even accused me of having designs on you."

"Did I really say that?"

"You know quite well that you did."

"Well, I didn't mean to sound such a coxcomb. It was rude and I apologise."

"I accept your apology, but it does not have the effect of making me regard you as a possible husband."

"Now I shall have to risk being rude again and point out that it is normal for a woman to wait until a man has made an offer before rejecting him. It's a small point, but I thought it as well to mention it."

In the darkness she blushed with mortification.

"Oh, how glad you must be that I gave you the chance to say that!" she smouldered.

"Well, you must admit that until then I was getting the worst of it," he observed mildly.

"You know very well what I meant. You'd said the Prince as good as told you to propose to me – "

"No, he didn't go quite as far as that," he said soothingly. "He knows how difficult I am to please."

There was a sulphurous silence before Rowena said,

"I suppose I know how to understand that."

"I am quite sure you do. One thing I did find admirable about you was the sharpness of your wits."

"Even though you considered that I didn't know how to behave like a lady?" she snapped.

"You must own to having been a little incautious."

"Splendid. Then all you need do is tell the Prince that my shocking behaviour makes me quite beneath you."

"Ah, but your shocking behaviour need not be a

problem to me. All I have to do is lock you in a high tower as soon as we're married, and make sure that the world never sees you again, thus leaving me free to live on your money."

"I beg your pardon!" she said scarcely able to believe her ears.

"After all, where would I find such another heiress? Your father's fortune has to be considered before I make any rash decisions."

"You – ?"

Incensed, Rowena turned on him, but then she saw the gleam of humour in his eyes. It transformed his normally stern face.

"You are making fun of me," she breathed.

"You goose, of course I am. What else is there to do but laugh at the fix we're in? I'm not really making fun of you, just the whole situation. It's difficult for both of us, and I can't but feel that dramatic gestures should be avoided. Mostly for your sake. I dare say your father could make himself very unpleasant."

"He certainly does love to have his own way," Rowena mused.

"Yes, we have to be subtle here. If we make it too plain that neither of us is remotely interested in marrying the other, we may give offence by our bluntness. So we should let them realise gradually that nothing will come of it."

"But will they? Papa can be very stubborn."

"So can I. Nothing on earth can induce me to propose to a woman once I've decided not to. Never fear. You are quite safe."

"Thank you," she said in a hollow voice.

"Now I think we may safely return to the others."

CHAPTER FOUR

The Duke led her to the saloon below deck where they rejoined the rest of the guests, who were all enjoying the party. A small party of gentlemen, including the Prince and Colonel Thornhill, had retired to a small saloon to play cards, but after a while they returned.

Rowena had fallen into conversation with some girls of her own age, and saw the Duke, on the other side of the room, talking seriously with her father and the Prince.

At last it was time to leave. Being royalty, the Prince of Wales departed first. The Duke took his leave of the Colonel and Rowena with a slight bow.

"Until tomorrow," he said.

"What did he mean, Papa?" Rowena wanted to know.

"He was so interested in *The Adventurer* that I invited him to join us on board tomorrow."

"Oh Papa, you didn't!"

"Certainly I did. Why ever not? He was most interested. Come now, let us be going back to the hotel. Sleep well, and up with the lark, for tomorrow is a busy day."

"Papa, I know what you're doing and it won't work."

"Doing? I am at a loss to understand you."

"You're trying to match me with the Duke of Wenfield, and I won't have it."

"Aren't you being a little impetuous, my dear? You've

only just met him."

Since it was now too late to tell her father about her two previous meetings with the Duke, this left Rowena in a quandary.

Nor could she tell him that they had discussed marriage to each other and decided to avoid it at all costs. Papa would be horrified at her lack of delicacy.

'But he'll be even more horrified that you're defying him,' whispered a little voice.

"We'll just have a pleasant day tomorrow, and think of nothing else."

"It won't be a pleasant day if I'm with him," she said fiercely. "I do not like him."

"Rowena, what are you saying? Did the Duke behave improperly while you were alone? Did he dare to – ?"

"No, he didn't. We walked the deck, arm in arm, and he made no attempt to – to – behave improperly."

"He didn't put his arm about you, or try to kiss you?"

"Certainly not!"

He sighed. "Ah well!"

Aghast, Rowena realised that Papa was actually disappointed. If the Duke had tried to compromise her, he might be forced to marry her. That was what the Colonel was thinking.

Was there anything he wouldn't do to see a coronet on her head? Even if it meant marrying her to the rudest, most obnoxious man in the world?

It was time to fight back.

Suddenly she put her hand to her head and leaned back with a sigh.

"What is it, my dear?" the Colonel asked solicitously.

"Nothing much Papa, just a headache. Parties sometimes do that to me."

"Aha, too much jollity!" he said roguishly. "A good night's sleep will put you right."

In bed that night Rowena thought rebelliously, 'I won't go. I won't go. Why did the Duke of Wenfield agree to this voyage after all we'd said? Perhaps it wasn't his fault, if the Prince was there, listening. But if he can't put a stop to it, then I will.'

She had no intention of spending a day out at sea, in company with a man who'd made it so rudely clear that he had no interest in her.

*

The next morning she didn't get out of bed. Her rebellion had begun. She would simply be too ill for the voyage.

Jenny carried her message to Colonel Thornhill that she was ailing, and he hurried to see her for himself.

"I'm sorry, Papa," she said. "But my headache is much, much worse."

Her father looked at her suspiciously, almost as though she were a malingering recruit in his regiment.

"The Duke would find me very poor company today," she said.

As she'd hoped, this was the deciding argument. However disappointed he might be, the Colonel wouldn't risk the Duke seeing her when she wasn't at her best.

"Very well, my dear," he said. "Keep to your bed today, and I hope you'll be better soon."

She knew a slight pang of guilt at deceiving him, but she couldn't see that he'd left her any choice.

More importantly, it would send a clear message to the Duke of Wenfield, that while he might feel obliged to go through a pantomime of social engagements that threw them together, she was made of sterner stuff.

She lay in bed until she heard him leave, then she rose and went to the window. From here she could just make out the harbour and the masts of *The Adventurer*. After a while they began to move. She sat there watching until the boat was at sea.

She spent a dull morning in bed. With nothing to do she began to brood.

Papa might be baulked this time, but he was a resourceful soldier, and would come again. Who knew what plans he might have made to throw her into the Duke of Wenfield's company next day? Or the day after? She couldn't stay in bed with a headache for ever.

At last she made up her mind, sat up in bed and rang the bell.

"We're leaving," she told Jenny when she arrived.

"Leaving miss? But where?"

"Back to Haverwick Castle. I feel my headache getting much worse, and I don't want to be ill in a hotel. I shall go home and retire to my room. I'll leave a letter for my father. Call a carriage, not our own landau, but hire some small, closed conveyance from the hotel."

She dressed quickly in travelling clothes, and wrote a letter to the Colonel saying much what she'd told Jenny. She left him in no doubt that she was preparing from a long period of withdrawal from society. She left Mrs. Kilton behind to finish packing up her gorgeous clothes and jewels, and follow after. She was determined to escape without delay.

In the hotel's closed carriage, she was able to close the doors, pull down all the blinds and travel unseen.

"Oh miss," Jenny wailed. "Are you dying?"

"Don't be absurd," Rowena chided her kindly. "I'm only – " she checked herself and hastily amended, "I'm only suffering from a very bad headache that will make it impossible for me to entertain."

"Too ill for parties, miss?"

"I'm afraid so."

"Or to wear your pretty dresses?"

"Too ill for that."

"Or to entertain the Duke, miss?" Jenny listened to all the gossip.

"Definitely too ill for that," Rowena declared.

In an hour they had reached Haverwick Castle, and Rowena retired to her room with a large pot of tea, a plate of cream cakes and a good novel. She needed some way to pass the time in what was clearly going to be a tedious wait.

The day wore on. As afternoon passed into evening, she braced herself for her father's appearance, or possibly a furious message from Dover demanding her instant return. But there was no message.

At last Mr. Farley looked in.

"Are you all right, my darling?" he asked tenderly.

"Of course I am, Grandpapa. You know there's nothing really the matter with me. I just want to escape that terrible man."

"This Duke of Wenfield sounds like a monster," Mr. Farley said, wide-eyed. "Oh my dear girl, you may count on my support and protection."

"Thank you, Grandpapa."

Rowena hugged him, but it went through her mind that she must rely on herself more than on her gentle grandfather.

"I wonder what Papa will do when he finds me gone," she mused. "He'll be so angry. Will he come rushing over here?"

"I've had an idea," said Mr. Farley. "I'll go to the hotel now and talk to him, tell him how poorly you are."

"But then he'll be angry with you."

Her grandfather chuckled. "He won't, you know. In his heart he's afraid of me. You'll see."

He was as good as his word, departing for Dover and returning two hours later to say that the Colonel had not returned.

"But there's no cause for alarm. Before he set sail he sent a message back to the hotel to say that his journey might go over until tomorrow, or even the day after. So you're safe for a while." He kissed her. "Goodnight, my dearest."

Full of relief, Rowena snuggled down and went to sleep.

But before she slept she spared a thought for the Duke, trapped on board *The Adventurer* with her father, for two days.

And she couldn't suppress a chuckle.

*

She spent the next day pleasantly. In the morning she had a gentle game of tennis with Grandpapa, and when he took his afternoon nap she wandered about in the gardens, thinking how nice it was to have no social duties.

But her enjoyment was short lived. Soon a powdered footman appeared, looking very strange among the greenery.

"Miss Rowena," he said, "your father has sent me to fetch you."

"He's here?"

"The Colonel arrived a few minutes ago, miss." The footman lowered his voice and said respectfully. "The Duke of Wenfield is with him."

Rowena's eyes flashed. How dare this man pursue her to her own home, when he knew what she thought of him?

She was finished, she decided, with being paraded before men with titles as though she was a prize animal at an agricultural show. This time she would simply refuse.

"That settles it," she said rebelliously. "I'm far too busy to come."

"You wish me to convey this message to the Colonel, miss?" the footman enquired woodenly.

A little of her courage seeped away.

"Couldn't you just say you couldn't find me?"

"As you wish."

He departed, with vast dignity.

When he was out of sight, she began to run in the direction of the stream that ran through the estate. Anywhere, to escape the net that was closing around her.

She found some children playing with a ball near the water. Nearby, their fathers, estate workers, were pruning trees. She waved to them, and joined in the game with the youngsters, who were tossing a ball back and forth, while a little dog barked with delight and tried to catch it.

It was a relief to take part in such an innocent pastime, and forget what might be waiting for her.

Gradually, as she chased and laughed, she found that her mind had calmed down. A new plan was evolving to meet this new situation.

The Duke had as good as told her that she couldn't be a Duchess because she didn't know how to behave in society.

Very well! She would show him. When she returned to the house she would act with great dignity, like the fine lady her father wanted her to be. She would not deviate one jot from the insipid rules of etiquette. That would silence his criticism, and make him realise that he had rejected her too soon.

Absorbed in her thoughts she missed the ball when it flew towards her. It went soaring into the air and landed in the river. The children set up a cry of protest, and one of the boys tried to dart into the water, but Rowena stopped him.

"No," she said firmly, "the water might be deep, I

think I can get it, using this tree."

A tree on the bank had grown low, so that one thick branch ran out over the water, trailing leaves. The ball had drifted against these leaves and for the moment was motionless. But she knew she must be quick, before it floated away.

Taking her shoes off she climbed onto the branch and began to edge her way along. She wobbled a good deal, but there were always minor branches to hold on to.

"Come on, come on," the children shouted encouragement.

Just a little bit further, just a little bit...

The branch was getting narrower and shakier under her. It was harder to keep her balance, but she wasn't going to be defeated.

And then disaster struck.

Her father and another man appeared from between the trees. She saw annoyance in the Colonel's face at the sight that met his eyes. Rowena saw that, but what she also saw, with dreadful clarity, was the face of his companion.

The Duke of Wenfield.

For one appalled moment their eyes held, hers full of shock, his full of cool, ironic amusement. Then she tried to straighten up and lost her footing. The next moment she'd toppled into the water.

It wasn't as deep as she had thought. In fact she could stand up easily and the water only came up to her waist. But she was horribly conscious of how she must look to him, with her hair plastered to her head and her thin white blouse made transparent by the water. Why, she wasn't decent, she realised with horror, and hastily crossed her arms over her chest.

She could have screamed with vexation. Only the moment before she'd been planning to impress him with her grand manners. Now there he was, standing on the bank regarding her ironically.

And here she was, Miss Thornhill, the heiress, the fine lady.

Looking like a drowned rat!

"Papa!" she said weakly.

The Colonel seemed incapable of speech or movement. For a moment it seemed as though he might explode.

The Duke moved first, coming down to the water's edge and reaching out a hand to her.

"Allow me," he said.

"No thank you," Rowena said quickly, backing towards the other bank. "I am in no danger, in fact – please go away."

She could hear herself sounding like a mannerless schoolgirl, but she was so embarrassed and mortified that she scarcely knew what she was saying.

"My daughter does not mean what she says," her father hastened to say.

"Oh, I think she knows her own mind very well," the Duke said coolly. "I can see that my presence must be unwelcome to her."

He bowed and walked away. The Colonel threw Rowena one glowering glance that promised it would be the worse for her, and hurried to follow him.

Rowena took a deep breath, thinking she must be the unluckiest person in the world.

She managed to return to the house by a route that avoided them, and ran upstairs as fast as she could.

Mrs Kilton exclaimed at the sight of her.

"Your Papa's here with the Duke of Wenfield, and a crowd of guests arriving later, and look at you!" she exclaimed.

In a moment she had maids flying about trying to fulfil a dozen orders at once. The Colonel planned to have bathrooms installed in the castle, but so far there had been no time, so one maid dragged out a hip bath while two others scampered to fetch hot water. Rowena scrubbed off the river water, while Mrs. Kilton laid out the clothes she considered suitable for the occasion.

But Rowena vetoed them all.

"I will wear something plain and dull," she said firmly.

"You do not possess anything plain and dull," her dresser said indignantly.

Rowena set her chin stubbornly. "I want to look twenty years older."

In the end the best she could manage was a dress of gold coloured twilled silk. The bottom of the skirt was trimmed with black velvet. Sleeves and waist also had black velvet trimmings, and there was a black silk sash.

"Now you will do my hair as plainly as possible," Rowena commanded. "No frills, no curls, no ribbons."

Mrs Kilton gave a little scream.

"I never heard of such a thing. Do you want to end up an old maid?"

"*Yes!*"

Mrs. Kilton was forced to give in, though with much weeping and wailing about her reputation if anyone thought she was responsible for this disaster.

When Rowena was satisfied that her appearance was as drab as could be managed, she went down the stairs in as stately and dignified a manner as she could.

When the Duke of Wenfield saw her looking like this, he would forget what she had looked like in the river.

In the hall she met her father.

"We have guests arriving or I should have spoken to you sooner," he said in a low, angry voice. "How dare you behave in such a way! First you feign illness to escape the voyage. Then I arrive back at the hotel to find you gone. And then – this morning – "

"I'm sorry, Papa, but I didn't know you would have the Duke with you."

"He is here as my guest and – what on earth do you mean by looking like that?"

"I am dressed with propriety, Papa."

"You look as ugly as a witch," he said flatly.

She could not resist saying, "Oh no, Papa. As long as I have your money behind me, men will never find me ugly."

At that moment she spotted the Duke of Wenfield out of the corner of her eye. It was hard to know how long he'd been there, but from his sudden grin she assumed he'd probably heard her last remark.

"Miss Thornhill," he said, coming forward, "allow me to hope that you have recovered from your unfortunate fall into the water."

"Thank you," she said stiffly. "I believe I must go and greet our guests."

"Of course. But you will permit me the honour of escorting you in to lunch."

There was no way to refuse him, so she smiled and agreed, but in her heart she was very angry with him. Why could this man not take a hint?

Carriages were arriving. The lunch party had been arranged quickly, and the Colonel had called on as many local dignitaries as he could find. The vicar, a mayor, and a neighbour who owned race horses, all with their wives.

Rowena went out to meet them, smiled charmingly, and welcomed them to the house.

The lofty butler announced that luncheon was served,

and the Duke stepped forward to offer her his arm. As they walked into the dining room together he murmured,

"It is quite useless, Miss Thornhill."

"I fail to understand you, sir."

"Trying to make yourself look plain. You are bound to fail. You are still the most beautiful woman here."

"I am not," she said firmly.

"I say you are."

"I am not."

"I am a connoisseur."

"Yes, you have already informed me that women chase you for your title, so you must have many opportunities to judge. But in my case you are mistaken."

"Do not argue with me, Miss Thornhill. I am never mistaken."

The Colonel's expensive French chef had excelled himself, and there were murmurs of admiration for the food. Despite this Rowena found herself feeling very uncomfortable.

Her attack on her own looks had succeeded far too well, and she caught more than one puzzled glance from her guests. Clearly they were wondering about this dowdy creature, and thinking she needed every possible help from her father's money to get a husband.

Sometimes they looked at the Duke, and Rowena was angrily certain that they were thinking he must be desperate for money to be here at all, paying attention to this dull young woman.

She could have screamed with vexation at having made such a stupid mistake.

It was all the Duke's fault, she thought. If he hadn't behaved so unreasonably, she wouldn't have had to put herself in this position. Really, there was no enduring the man.

After lunch came an insufferably tedious afternoon, showing her guests around the house and the grounds. The Duke accompanied them, the very picture of gentlemanly interest. Which, she thought bitterly, was exactly the kind of behaviour one might have expected from him.

"May we not take a little stroll down to the stream?" he asked. "It looks so pretty from here."

"You have already seen the stream," she reminded him.

"But your other guests have not, and the house is shown to its best advantage from down there. Water improves a landscape so much, don't you think? And one may always hope to see a water nymph."

"Really?" she said frostily. "Personally I have never seen a water nymph, and I don't believe they exist."

"Certainly they do. I saw one myself only recently, and it's a sight I shall never forget."

Then he was button-holed by the mayor's wife, who professed a deep interest in 'unseen presences'. She interrogated him on this subject all the way to the stream and back, and to do him justice, Rowena thought, he bore it very well.

Just the same, she felt that he'd come by his just deserts.

*

When it came to dressing for the evening, Rowena did not repeat her experiment of the afternoon. Her father would demand that she look her best, and she too had no further desire to be thought dowdy.

So she allowed Mrs. Kilton to attire her in an evening gown of very thin white muslin over blue silk. It was decorated with deep puffing around the hem, and at the back were three garlands of blue flowers.

Her hair was dressed in little curls and adorned with

tiny blue flowers, matching the ones on the dress. Sapphires hung from her ears and about her neck. Her mirror told her that she was lovely, but was it herself or her fabulous jewels that people looked at?

Tonight they were entertaining some members of the Clipper Club who had driven over from Dover for the occasion. Here were the titles that the Colonel loved to entertain. Although only the Duke of Wenfield was actually staying in the house, there would be two Viscounts, a Baronet and a knight at his table tonight.

'And that's all he thinks of,' she brooded. 'Titles, money, social advancement. If only I could escape before this goes any further. But what can I do? Where could I go?'

After the meal there was to be a 'musical entertainment'. The Colonel had engaged a well known operatic soprano to sing sentimental ballads. As she sat listening, Rowena was aware of interested glances being cast in her direction, and that of the Duke.

No doubt everyone was expecting an announcement. She felt the net closing around her.

When the recital was over, the pianist strummed on the piano while the guests began an impromptu dance.

"Will you dance with me, Miss Thornhill?" the Duke asked her.

"Thank you, sir, but I prefer not to dance."

"As you wish. We shall have plenty of time for talking over the next few days."

"But – aren't you leaving tomorrow?"

"Not at all. Your father has invited me for another week, and I have accepted."

She rose to her feet. "I think we should dance."

As they circled the floor, she said, "I fail to understand you, sir. We are agreed, are we not, that we will not tolerate this attempt to match us? So why are you staying?"

"Your Papa has promised me some excellent shooting. Whatever efforts he may make to pair us off will not succeed, so I suggest that we simply forget the matter."

"You know very well that isn't possible, with everyone looking at us. They are doing so now."

"Yes, I'm rather afraid they are. Let's get out of their sight."

Before she could suspect what he meant to do, he whirled her out of the French windows onto the terrace.

"This just makes it worse," she exclaimed crossly.

"You mean they'll think I brought you here to kiss you? Don't worry, I promise not to."

"Beware my lord, the net that closes about me will also close about you. Then we'll both be in a fix."

"We'll have to think of a way of extricating ourselves."

"I'd hoped you were going to do that, but I see it's all going to be left to me."

He laughed suddenly. "Do you know, you sound like a governess."

"I have a practical turn of mind, and it's very useful."

"I don't much care for practical women."

"Capital! Things couldn't be better!"

"And to think I once accused you of trying to lure me on! What was I thinking of?" exclaimed the Duke.

"Not of me, certainly. I've never tried to lure a man, and I never will."

"Then you've never been in love."

"Have you?" she asked, startled into curiosity.

"Oh yes. Many times."

"Many times? Then it was not true love, or it would last forever."

"You may be right," he said, sounding a little sad.

"The difficulty is – telling the difference at the time."

"I think you're a most improper person," she said, scandalised.

"True."

She knew she should insist on going inside. No lady could remain on a moonlit terrace with an improper person. But that could wait a little, she decided.

"Does this remind you of the evening we met at Ellesmere House?" he asked. "The dancing, the moonlight."

"But nothing else is the same. You concealed your identity."

"I wasn't hiding in the shadows, as you seem to suggest," he countered. "Lord Ellesmere is a friend of mine. We were at school together and I was paying him a short visit. I passed up the chance to attend the ball because I've attended too many, and spent the evening in the library.

"After a while I lost interest in my book and turned off the lamp. I went out for a walk in the garden, to enjoy the moonlight, and had just returned when you came flying in."

"And you immediately thought it was another trick to capture you. And then, of course, when I threw myself into your way on horseback, that decided you. I wonder what I would have to do to convince you that I am not part of my father's plan."

"You're a little unjust to me, I think. I'd have to be very foolish not to have understood the message you sent me by not coming on that voyage. Not that it was necessary after I'd made it so plain that you had nothing to fear from me."

"I dare say it's all a misunderstanding, and you don't need Papa's money at all," she said coolly.

"Oh no, I'm fairly poor."

"For a Duke!"

"For a Duke. I have a small house in this part of the

country that I must sell. That's why I'm down here at the moment. And there are other economies I must make. I shan't have to sell the Wenfield country seat, but there are some urgent repairs that need doing, especially in the turrets, where I seem to have bats."

Once more she had the disturbing sensation that he was teasing her.

"I do wish you would be serious," she scolded him.

"But my dear Miss Thornhill, bats in the turrets is a very serious matter."

"Then you do need an heiress."

"Of course. I've never denied needing an heiress. I merely promise that it won't be you."

They walked on in silence. She was unable to decide why his attitude was so annoying. She certainly didn't want him, but neither did she desire to be informed at every turn that he didn't want her.

"I hope you enjoy your trip aboard Papa's yacht," she said, to make conversation.

"Now you're being untruthful, Miss Thornhill. You hope no such thing. You would prefer us to have been bored to tears with each other's company, and to have learned our lesson so thoroughly that no-one will try to pressure us into marriage."

She took a deep breath. "Well, I may have been thinking something of the kind about Papa, because when he gets an idea in his head I might as well shout at the moon."

As if to prove it the Colonel appeared on the terrace before them, beaming.

"Well, well, we all wondered where the two of you had vanished."

Rowena inwardly groaned. It was as good as an announcement.

At the same time, she knew that if Papa hoped to trick

the Duke into an engagement by this kind of method, he was in for a disappointment. She might not like the Duke of Wenfield, but she recognised that he was nobody's fool.

He proved it now, sliding easily around the Colonel's clumsy attempt to back him into a corner, by leading them all back inside, and declaring himself ready for a game of cards.

After which all the men decided to play cards, leaving the women to talk among themselves. It was done very smoothly and skilfully.

'Well done!' Rowena thought.

It was the kindest thing she had thought of him all evening.

CHAPTER FIVE

It was two in the morning.

The house was dark and quiet.

The guests had gone. Those who remained had retired to their rooms to sleep.

Except for Rowena, who had no intention of sleeping.

Tonight she must make her escape. She would leave the house, and in the morning they would find her room empty.

It was drastic, but she saw no other way, of escaping the marriage with the Duke of Wenfield that was being slowly forced on her. Papa would brook no refusal, and whatever he might say, the Duke might not be able to resist all that money to deal with his bats.

She packed one bag. It was all she dared to take. Then she crept out of her room and headed for the stairs.

But she was pulled up short by the sound of voices coming from below. She recognised the housekeeper and the head butler, and slipped back into the shadows.

It was true that they didn't have the authority to stop her, but they could raise the alarm.

There was only one way open to her, and that was the tree outside her window.

As a child she'd been a tomboy, always climbing trees to Mama's horror. Looking out of the window she knew she could manage this tree, which had a thick trunk and plenty of heavy branches, some of which came close to the window.

She dropped her bag to the ground and heard the soft clunk as it landed. Then, hitching up her skirts, she climbed out of the window, tested her weight on a branch, and found it strong enough.

Moving carefully, she inched her way along until she could grasp another branch and use it to balance herself as she left the window behind.

Now she was right out in the tree, committed to the outrageous action of running away from home.

She took one look at the house, thinking there was still time to turn back.

But no! She had decided. It was time to demonstrate a strong mind.

She took another step down, and another. She was going to escape.

But then, as she slowly loosened her grip on the branch above her, she felt something give beneath her. There was an ominous cracking sound. She floundered, seeking somewhere for her foot to land. There was nowhere.

Then she was falling – falling to earth – falling in darkness.

She braced herself for a terrible crash landing, broken bones, perhaps death.

But when her fall stopped suddenly she wasn't on the ground.

She was in two strong arms, held firmly against a broad, masculine chest, while above her head an exasperated masculine voice was saying,

"Really Miss Thornhill, you cannot spend the entire rest of your life running away from me. It grows tedious."

*

"You must have taken leave of your senses," he thundered. "What kind of bird-brained, feather-headed – "

"There is no need to insult me," Miss Thornhill said crossly.

"It is not insulting you to state the plain facts."

They were in the conservatory, where the Duke had lingered for a final cigar. He had been about to go to bed, when the sound of a bag landing on the ground had alerted him, and he'd gone outside just in time to catch Rowena as she fell.

The Duke wasted no time taking her indoors, fetching her bag, then returning and locking the conservatory door, enclosing them both. But he did not put on the light, being unwilling to attract attention.

"If I hadn't been there you might be dead by now," he said furiously. "And if you had escaped – where were you going?"

"It doesn't matter."

"There's no such place as 'it doesn't matter'. You can't go there. You've got to be somewhere, and you've got to have a good explanation. And money. Have you any?"

"I have some jewellery to sell."

"Wonderful! You should have tried that. Then, instead of catching you from a tree I could have rescued you from a police station. Then we probably would have been compromised."

"Not in a million years," she said vehemently. "You are the last man I would ever marry."

"If you continue to play fast and loose with your reputation, I'll probably be the last man you'll have the chance to marry."

"Then I'll stay an old maid. Anything would be better than you."

"My sentiments exactly, madam."

"Then why don't you give me a little help?" she cried. "You say you're as reluctant as I am, but all the work is left to me. Why couldn't you have just gone away tomorrow?"

"Because I'm making plans to rent your father's yacht. I thought a cruise would take me away for several weeks and you would no longer be in any danger from me. But there are talks, negotiations, that will take some days. Then I'll be gone and trouble you no more."

She sighed. "I wish I had known that."

Something forlorn in her voice made him stop his pacing and look at her more closely in the half light. A gentler expression came over his face.

"Perhaps I haven't been very clever about this," he said, sitting beside her. "I forget that it's worse for you than for me. A man can always simply leave."

"But if a girl tries to leave everything goes wrong," she said in a wobbly voice.

"Come now, you're not going to cry are you? You've been so strong up until now."

"I don't mean to cry, but I've nowhere to turn for help."

Then he surprised her. Taking both her hands in his he said, "You can turn to me."

"No, how can I?" she said with a shaky laugh. "You're the one I'm running away from."

He considered this. "I think you should stop doing that. It doesn't work. It's better if we're on the same side. You're right, I should have been helping you, and I've done very badly. Will you forgive me for my clumsiness, and let us start again, as friends? As brother and sister if you like."

How kind and warm his voice was, and how strong his hands holding hers. Suddenly she didn't dislike him any more. If he would be her friend and brother, then there was hope.

"I've always wanted a brother," she said shyly.

"Do you realise," he said seriously, "that we are the only two in the world who can solve each other's problems? For mine are the same as yours, with family pressure to make a marriage that takes no account of my feelings."

"Of course I wasn't meant to be the Duke at all. It was supposed to be my cousin James. But even as a mere cousin, I was told repeatedly that it was my duty to marry in a way that brings credit to the family. Either a lady with a title or a rich father. Preferably both, of course, but at least one or the other.

"James and I used to commiserate with each other, because of course it was worse for him. They actually managed to engage him to a titled lady, and when he died last year, before the marriage could take place, one of my uncles had the confounded impudence to suggest that she would 'do for me'."

Rowena gasped in horror.

"These people have no heart," she cried.

"No heart at all," he agreed. "Luckily she was a strong minded lady and would have none of it. She was secretly in love with an attorney, and wasn't prepared to see her happiness snatched away a second time. They eloped, and I gather are extremely happy.

"I believe she was right in following her heart," he continued. "It's what I want to do myself."

"But I thought you had to have an heiress?"

"I was teasing you. I'll manage without the heiress. There are some pictures I can sell, and I will, rather than relinquish my dream of marrying a woman who loves me for myself alone, without thought of my title. There! Now I've confided to you what I've told nobody else. The others would have laughed at me. Only you, my dear sister and friend, can understand."

He was still holding her hand. Suddenly Rowena tightened her own fingers, and laid her other hand over his.

"Then we are the only ones who can help each other," she said.

"I shall help you at once by taking myself off on a voyage."

"Why that's it!" exclaimed Rowena. *"That's the answer to our problem."*

In a blinding flash an idea had come to her, and it seemed as though heaven itself had inspired her, just as she'd longed for.

"You think my going away will solve everything?" the Duke asked.

"We'll both go."

He stared at her, as though afraid she'd become light headed. Then he said ironically,

"Won't that land us in exactly the kind of trouble we're both trying to avoid?"

"Not if we go about it the right way," Rowena said excitedly. "You will tell Papa you want to hire *The Adventurer* and take some friends on a cruise around the Mediterranean. You will invite me to join the party, as an act of courtesy towards him."

The Duke stared at her. Then he said:

"What would you and I gain by that?"

"Wait, let me tell you the rest. You would ask the men, who are to be your guests, and I would ask the women. Perhaps the men should have titles, not as important as yours, but it would certainly help if there was another Duke on board."

"That may be a little difficult," he observed. "Unmarried Dukes are in rather short supply. And why must they have titles?"

"Because we're looking for men who are being pursued in the marriage market for their status. Just like you. Mind you, if they were untitled but rich, I suppose that might do just as well."

"You're very kind. And the girls?"

"I'm not the only girl being pushed by an ambitious parent. I know several others who will be glad to make their escape. On our voyage they will feel free. They will not be harried. No parents will be invited."

There was silence for a moment. Then the Duke said slowly:

"I see what you are trying to do. Do you really believe it is possible?"

"I not only think it's possible, but I believe some of our friends will fall in love when they no longer feel under pressure. What could be more romantic than being at sea, free from all the social bonds they have at home?"

"It is certainly an idea," the Duke admitted. "Do you think your father will let me hire the yacht?"

"Of course he will," Rowena replied. "When he knows I'm going he'll expect us to tell him the good news immediately we arrive home. Of course we won't have any news to announce, since we're really doing this to get away from each other – if you see what I mean."

"I think I can follow that," he said dryly.

"In fact, you will probably return engaged to one of my friends."

"If I do, will you send her your condolences?" he asked with a twinkle.

"Oh, don't remind me of what I said that day."

"But it's one of my favorite memories. How you can possibly want to be trapped on a ship with a 'conceited, boorish, mannerless creature who doesn't know how to behave like a gentleman'?"

"I said that before I knew you properly," she told him severely.

"Ah! I see."

"Now that I've met you, I think you're *much* worse than that."

His eyes gleamed appreciation. "Touché, Miss Thornhill! I shall have to be on my guard."

"You need not despair," Rowena said demurely. "Whoever you fall in love with, I promise not to spoil things by telling her the truth about you."

"That's very kind of you. But suppose I don't fall in love with any of your friends."

"I really think you should try to," she advised him earnestly. "Otherwise my father will start trying to match us again."

He nodded. "And that is to be avoided at all costs."

Suddenly Rowena sighed.

"Oh, what does it matter what happens when it's over?" she asked. "At the very least we'll have a breathing space. At the best we may have the satisfaction of making one or two of our friends really happy, because they have found the love we are all seeking."

She spoke softly with a little quiver in her voice, which told the Duke it meant a great deal to her.

He had released her hand, but now he took it again and spoke with gentle seriousness.

"I think your idea is inspired, and you can rely on me to do everything you wish about this voyage. If we can bring it off, perhaps our friends may be happy. Perhaps you or I will find, among the guests, the true love we seek. Perhaps both of us will. We must protect and care for each other as brothers and sisters do."

"Oh, yes," breathed Rowena. "We must do that."

He raised her hand to his lips and kissed it. It was not a loverlike gesture, but a solemn pledge of friendship and trust.

For a long moment they sat in silence, each understanding the silent pledge that had been given.

After a while he said,

"I have promised to do as you wish. Do you have any other ideas for our voyage?"

"We would need a chaperone, otherwise the girls' parents will say their reputations have been ruined." She looked at him cheekily. "Then you might have to marry all of them."

"This begins to sound dangerous," he mused.

"You must think of someone respectable enough to satisfy the parents, but who won't interfere in any way with what we are doing."

"An impossible combination! No, wait! I know exactly the person we need. My aunt, a delightful lady. She ran away from home when she was only eighteen and married a curate, much to her father's fury."

His voice dropped as he added: "I believe they were blissfully happy until he was sent overseas, doubtless by the Bishop. It was there he died of some obscure disease, which he caught when tending to the sick and dying."

"How sad," Rowena replied. "Was she very miserable?"

"She was broken-hearted," the Duke told her. "Because of her history, she is the one relation of mine who understands what I am looking for in marriage."

"I think she sounds very brave and of course you are quite right, she would be the ideal person for us. She would understand our feelings as no one else would."

"I think you must be the most original young lady I've ever met," he said admiringly.

"Well, my Lord – "

"Do you not think you could call me Mark?" he asked. "Not in your father's hearing of course, because it would awaken his expectations. But when we are alone."

"Very well, and you must call me Rowena, on the same conditions. I was simply going to say that I think it will be good for you to meet a number of girls, who aren't standing on your doorstep wanting you to ask them in."

"The only person standing on my doorstep," the Duke said, "is your father. I am not a fool. I realise he's been trying to display his wealth to me."

"In other words he is tempting you," Rowena said. "I expect a lot of your friends have been tempted too. I suppose every mother and father starts the season by hoping their daughter will marry tremendously well – either wealth or a title. It's as you said, 'preferably both, but at least one or the other.' Most of them must be very disappointed when July comes, and the season is over."

"They shouldn't be so greedy," the Duke said. "Money isn't everything in life, even though most people think it is. You can't buy love in hard cash."

"Of course not," Rowena agreed. "It comes from the heart, or as the Russians say: 'from the heart and the soul.'"

"Obviously you've considered this seriously," the Duke said. "And you are absolutely right."

"But we must be careful how we explain ourselves to the others," Rowena mused. "I'll tell the girls this is a chance to be free, and enjoy being amongst people of our own age."

The Duke smiled. "Then they'll certainly accept your invitation."

"No your invitation," Rowena said. "Make no mistake, this is *your* party and that's how we must present it."

"Why must it be my party and not yours?"

"Because at all costs we must appear respectable."

He raised his eyebrows satirically in a way she found subtly disturbing.

"Appear? Aren't you respectable Rowena?"

"I'm nineteen," she said with dignity. "That's too young to be respectable in the sense I mean."

"Oh, you mean respectable as in 'fuddy-duddy'?"

"Yes. Now you're much older than me – "

"I'm thirty," he said stiffly, "not that much older."

"But old enough to be respectable – "

"Fuddy-duddy."

"Well a little fuddy-duddy is what we need," she said, wondering why he was suddenly being so difficult. "You've even got a few grey hairs coming at the side."

"All my family go grey early. My father was completely white by the time he was forty-five. I may add that it did not prevent women finding him irresistible."

'Of course not,' she thought. 'If he'd looked anything like his son he must have been even more handsome and distinguished with white hair than with dark.' She wondered how Mark would look at that age.

"He led my poor mother a terrible dance with his flirtations," Mark continued

Then he seemed to pull himself hurriedly together. "I shouldn't be telling you this, it's most improper. I merely wanted to point out that a couple of grey hairs do not mean I'm staggering towards an early grave."

"I never said it did. I merely felt they might be useful in giving you a – a *settled* appearance."

"Thank you," he said, chagrined. "Well, it seems to me you have no problem. Just tell your father he can forget about matching us, as I am much too old for you."

"Only eleven years," Rowena said innocently. "Lord

Toston was eighteen years older than me and Papa said – "

"Perhaps we could change the subject," the Duke asked, with a stiff smile.

"Very well. I didn't mean to offend you. Of course I can see you *are* offended, although I can't think why."

"No, I'm sure you can't," the Duke said, recovering his temper and regarding her with amusement. "But that's because you're very young. At nineteen I dare say thirty does seem ancient."

"Not really, but I can understand why your family wants you to take a wife without delay," she said wisely.

"Before I'm on crutches, you mean?" he asked with a grin.

"You're making fun of me."

"Only a little. I take your point about being respectable. Perhaps I could put a little flour on my temples to increase my – er – settled appearance?"

"Nonsense! Nonsense! Flour doesn't work!"

The Duke and Rowena both turned, startled by the voice that had come out of the shadows.

"Who's there?" the Duke demanded.

"I am," said Mr. Farley, coming forward. "I slipped into the conservatory some time ago. I've been standing here listening, and a more bird-brained scheme I've never heard."

He came out where they could see him more clearly. He had a glass of champagne in one hand and a cream cake in the other, and had evidently been plundering the remains of the party.

"A pack of young people all together on the ocean," he said, "flirting, laughing, making eyes at each other, hanky panky – "

"There isn't going to be any hanky-panky," the Duke said at once. "Miss Thornhill is too young and innocent, and

I'm too old and fuddy-duddy. We've decided that."

"I didn't say you were old – " Rowena said quickly.

"Of course he isn't," Mr. Farley said robustly. "Prime of life. Hale and hearty young man."

"I've got a grey hair," the Duke offered.

"I don't care if you've got a headfull of grey hairs," Mr. Farley said. "A man of thirty is still young and vigorous, and just right for a girl of nineteen."

"If you mean Miss Thornhill, we're doing this to avoid having to marry each other," the Duke reminded him.

Farley gave him a level gaze. "Are you?" he said evenly. "Are you indeed!"

The Duke couldn't meet his eyes.

"Well you'll have to do a great deal better than flour," Mr. Farley went on. "I tried it when I was a young curate, preaching to people old enough to be my grandparents. Never did any good. One old dowager told me to go away and not come back until I'd washed my hair."

"But we have the Duke's aunt as chaperone," Rowena said anxiously. "Surely that will do?"

"One old lady? Not enough. She can't be everywhere. Two chaperones would be better. And if one of them was a clergyman – "

"The perfect answer," the Duke said with a grin. "Why didn't we think of it?"

"Oh Grandpapa, would you really come?"

"I think I'd better, m'dear. For one thing, if I'm there I can stop your father trying to come too."

Rowena was ecstatic.

"Dearest Grandpapa. It's so sweet of you to sacrifice yourself like this for us."

Mr. Farley had the grace to blush. "Nothing I do for you is too much trouble, m'dear."

*

The following morning the Colonel found his daughter in the morning room, where she was writing.

She was half afraid he would demand what she meant by being up half the night, but one glance at his face told her she was safe. Last night had ended with the three of them climbing the stairs and creeping to their rooms through the darkened house. Once Rowena had closed her bedroom window, there was no evidence of her attempted escape.

She hadn't met the Duke at breakfast as he'd gone out for a stroll. Deliberately, she suspected.

Now her father was full of news.

"I've just been having a long talk with the Duke," he said.

"Really Papa?" She opened her eyes as wide and innocently as she could.

"I must admit, my dear, that when he first asked to speak to me, I hoped he was making an offer for your hand, but it seems he has something quite different in mind. He wishes to hire *The Adventurer* to take his aunt on a sea voyage. It seems she's been ailing recently."

"That's very considerate of him, Papa."

"Yes, he seems to be an excellent young man. I only wish – but, no matter. If it cannot be, I suppose I must accept that. But I'm glad to see that you and he will still be friends."

"Papa," she laughed, "you have no subtlety. You mean you want him to introduce me to other young men in his circle."

"Well, I dare say he'll do that when he gets back to England," Colonel Thornhill said.

When he'd gone Rowena sat down, puzzled. Her father had made no mention of herself being one of the party. And that was very strange.

77

A moment later the Duke looked in, relieved to find her there.

"Has your father spoken to you yet?"

"Yes, but he seems to know nothing of my joining the party."

"I haven't mentioned it. It would have sounded suspicious, coming so soon. You must seem to be an afterthought. Leave everything to me."

He was gone.

'Poor Papa,' Rowena thought. 'It does seem terrible to deceive him like this, although I'm sure it's quite an innocent deception. I simply must lead my own life, and find love in my own way, without letting him take over. Mark is right. It's better if this seems to have nothing to do with me.'

Mark played his part with consummate skill. Having secured the ship he invited Mr. Farley.

"As company for my aunt," he explained to the Colonel. "She has a preference for clerical gentlemen, having been married to one."

His next master stroke was to bring his aunt to Haverwick Castle to meet Colonel Thornhill and his daughter. She turned out to be about seventy, with a long nose and a way of looking down it as though at worms. The few words she spoke implied that the world and everyone in it was insufferably tedious.

Rowena was astonished that this aloof, haughty woman could ever have noticed a curate, never mind married one.

She turned a puzzled gaze on Mark. He met her eyes blandly.

Then she gasped with shock.

He had winked at her.

How very improper!

But such fun!

The Colonel was in seventh heaven at being trodden on by the sister of a Duke. When the Lady Honoria announced that she positively doted on 'that dear child, Rowena' and insisted that she must accompany them on the voyage, the Colonel saw the door opening again to all his social ambitions.

He would have liked to invite himself along too, but when he ventured a hint Lady Honoria fixed him with her lorgnette until he faltered into silence.

At last Her Ladyship bade him a lofty farewell and departed into her nephew's care. Having taken her home he presented her with a huge box of her favourite chocolates, "for playing your part superbly".

CHAPTER SIX

After that things were easy. The presence of Lady Honoria and a clergyman laid a cloak of respectability over the party so completely, that some young people were inclined to refuse their invitations, and had to have the truth of the matter hurriedly explained to them.

In no time at all a lively young party was assembled.

When Rowena came to select her guests, she found she already had a mental list of girls who would benefit from this kind of trip. It was almost as though some secret part of her mind had been preparing for some time.

First she chose the Hon. Margaret Fleming, whom she liked and pitied. Margaret had a very pushy mother who was determined she should make an important marriage, and then be able to introduce her two younger sisters to well-born men.

But Margaret, although pretty, was too shy to take the town by storm, and when she still wasn't engaged at twenty-one her mother despised and bullied her. Rowena had discovered this when she stayed with the family for a few days. The two girls shared a bedroom, and she saw Margaret's tears.

"What can I do?" she'd wept. "If men don't want to marry me, why should they be pushed into it by Mama? If it comes to that, I don't want to marry them."

"One day you will find someone you love," Rowena had said encouragingly.

"I don't think so. I am not beautiful like you and Mama begrudges every penny she spends on me."

"But you are a lovely person," Rowena had told her. "Lots of men will think so."

"Well, they are very slow in coming forward," Margaret had answered bitterly.

Rowena had felt very sorry for Margaret, so she was first on her list.

Next was the Hon. Elaine Danver, an heiress, not as spectacularly rich as Rowena, but with two very pushy parents.

After much thought Rowena also included Lady Dulcie Sinclair. Her dowry was no more than reasonable, and since her father was an Earl she already knew the higher ranks of the aristocracy and didn't have to hunt for a title.

Her drawback was that she was horse mad and dog mad, and they were the only things she could discuss. To someone of the same inclination, she would be a perfect companion. To anybody else she would seem rather boring. Rowena liked her, although she too sometimes found Dulcie's conversation limited.

She still had one vacancy, when Mark came to discuss his own list with her.

"You'll like the Hon. Andrew Rackton," he said. "He's a cousin of my own. Lord Patrick Tellman is a good friend. I don't know Dominic Fears very well, but he has a lot of money and is expected to marry a title, which bores him a good deal."

"I'll probably get on well with him," Rowena mused. "Who's the last one."

"Lord Brice. He's an Earl."

"What a catch!" Rowena exclaimed excitedly.

"In some ways, yes, although he has his disadvantages."

He refused to explain further, but seemed to be enjoying a joke.

*

At last the great day came. Rowena and Mr. Farley, accompanied by her father, set off for Dover in the carriage, followed by a fourgon with all her luggage, and Jenny. Mrs. Kilton was a terrible sailor, and had had hysterics at the thought of going on board.

They arrived to find the others ahead of them and the ship already being boarded. The girls welcomed Rowena with shrieks of delight, and the men became very grave and sensible as they greeted the Colonel.

He came aboard to speak to Mark and look over his ship with pride.

"Take care of the ship," the Colonel told Mark. "It'll serve you well," he said. "I trust you'll have a fine voyage."

"I have every faith in the ship, and in its fine crew, sir," Mark responded. "Have no fear, I'll return everyone safely."

Rowena kissed her father goodbye.

"I hope you have a calm sea," he said, "otherwise there will be too many of your guests in bed."

"Oh, Papa, do not leave us on such a dismal note," Rowena protested. "There is nothing romantic in seasickness."

At the same time she was laughing. It seemed extraordinary that her ideas had really come true. They were actually on board *The Adventurer*.

Impulsively she said, "You have been wonderful, Papa, in letting me do this."

The Colonel eyed his child with a touch of cynicism.

"The party has developed a little from the one I agreed

to," he said. "It's become a lot livelier."

"Why Papa, how can you say such a thing, when we have Grandpapa and Lady Honoria – "

"And you and the Duke – "

"We are extra chaperones. But of course some of our friends may want to pair off, and come back blissfully happy."

"Never count your chickens before they are hatched," her father warned. "They may come back all hating each other and be glad to return to the security of England."

Rowena laughed. "You are making fun of me. The Duke and I are secretly having bets on how many of our guests will be engaged when we come back to England." Impulsively she threw her arms about her father.

"Thank you, thank you, for being so understanding and kind."

Her father smiled. "Well, take care of yourself, my darling," he said. "The house will be very lonely without you, so don't be away too long."

With a final kiss on his daughter's cheek, he walked down the gangway. Rowena leaned over to wave him goodbye.

"Thank you, Papa, and take care of yourself," she called. "I love you! I love you!"

Her father waved as the yacht began to move. The sound of the water splashing prevented them from saying any more to each other.

'We are really beginning our adventure,' Rowena said to herself, going below deck as the yacht moved out into the sea.

As she expected several of her guests were sitting in the saloon, celebrating with champagne. The Duke was amongst them.

When he saw Rowena he said. "Come and join us. We

are drinking to good health, good weather and good temper to start us off."

He handed her a glass of champagne, and they clinked glasses.

"We thought we could choose our cabins when we are out at sea," Mark said. "As it is your party and mine we have to decide which of us will have the master cabin."

"But I think your aunt should have it," Rowena replied.

"No, she prefers a smaller cabin and has gone below already to claim it." He looked around at everyone. "You understand that she will act as chaperone, so no one afterwards can say you were not looked after and prevented from misbehaving yourself."

They all laughed, and some of the men gave roguish glances at the women, who pretended to be very much shocked.

"Of course you must have the master cabin," Rowena insisted.

"Why of course?" the Duke wanted to know.

"Because men come first," she told him mischievously. "If you don't put them first they might feel disagreeable or sulky all the way there and back."

"I promise not to be disagreeable and sulky," he said at once.

She smiled. "And I promise I will be very happy in an ordinary cabin, without having to worry in case you think I am claiming to be more important than I really am."

"You need not be afraid of that," Mark answered. "Everyone here thinks they are very important and we have to treat them with respect, unless they become so disagreeable we have to push them overboard."

Everybody roared with laughter at this sally, and the steward went around refilling glasses.

Eventually when she went below, Rowena found she had a very attractive cabin decorated in pink which was her favourite colour. As it was quite large there was room for a truckle bed, for Jenny.

When she'd changed her clothes she joined the others on deck, where they were all discussing their living quarters.

Margaret and Elaine were sharing the cabin next door to Rowena, which exactly suited them, for they were good friends.

"We can talk at night, which I always enjoy, when I go to bed," said Elaine.

"We can say how much we dislike so-and-so," Margaret added, "and how much we like someone else."

"I have never heard anything so disgraceful," Rowena exclaimed. "You know as well as I do that everyone has to enjoy themselves on this trip.

"It's a journey of pleasure, perhaps even romance if we're very fortunate, and anyone who is disagreeable or unpleasant will be put ashore, and left to return home in disgrace."

There were shouts of laughter at this.

Then the Duke's cousin, Andrew, said,

"I thought there was a catch somewhere and if this is one way of getting rid of me, I will find some way of having my revenge."

As the boat moved out further into the channel, they crowded on deck, watching the sun on the water.

"What do you think of my selection?" Mark asked. "Didn't I choose some splendid young men for you?"

"They are not for me," she said firmly.

"But you must have first choice."

"If I carry one of them off, we'll have odd numbers and one girl in tears."

"Not at all. I promise to pay the odd girl a lot of attention, and that will even us up again."

"Suppose the girl isn't interested in you."

He grinned. "Then I'll have to exert myself to please her."

And he would know exactly how to do that, she thought. He was the most handsome man on board, and if he gave a young woman all his attention, she would probably soon find him the handsomest man in the world. And the most charming. And the most attractive, with that look he sometimes had in his eyes, as though he couldn't decide whether to flirt or laugh.

Not that he would be flirting with her, and she was very glad of it. She was quite decided on that point. Nothing could please her more than to know Mark had no romantic interest in her.

"Rowena – ?"

"I beg your pardon?"

"You were off in a dream."

"Was I? Do forgive me. How rude – "

"I'm not offended, but I'd give a deal to know what you were thinking about to bring that sparkle to your eyes."

"It's just a reflection of the water."

"I don't think so. You were thinking very pleasant thoughts then. They brought a half smile to your lips – "

"Indeed? Then I was probably thinking of one of the young men you brought on this voyage."

"I wonder if I can guess which one. What about Lord Brice?"

She gave a choke of laughter. Mark had warned her of poor Brice's disadvantages, and she had discovered that the young man, although handsome, rich and well born, was almost paralysed by nerves.

"Yes, it's definitely Brice," Mark grinned.

She pressed her lips together, refusing to answer him.

A little further along the deck she saw Jane Stanton, sad and alone. Jane's engagement to Francis Dillon, had recently been broken off, and Rowena had hastened to offer her the last vacant place.

She didn't know why the engagement had ended, because Jane couldn't discuss it without bursting into tears. She, normally so bright and merry, now stood in an unhappy dream, gazing out over the water.

As Rowena watched, Jane turned away, tears streaming down her face, and stumbled. It was Lord Brice who reached out to steady her. She apologised. He said it was his fault and produced a large clean handkerchief.

"Let's leave them to it," Mark murmured.

"There's another couple down there," Rowena said, pointing.

Lady Honoria had come out on deck, and was being squired by Mr. Farley. The two of them sat in deckchairs absorbed in conversation.

"She's quite different to what she seemed at first," said Rowena.

"Quite different," he agreed, with a smile.

"You've been very clever," she said. "Oh, I am so looking forward to this journey."

"I hope you don't get seasick in the Bay of Biscay. It can be quite choppy there, but the weather forecast for the next few days is good. We'll anchor off France tonight, and tomorrow, with any luck we might get right across the bay and south as far as Lisbon. We'll stop there for one night and then go on into the Mediterranean. After that we can go more slowly."

At Cherbourg they dropped anchor for the night, which meant that, to everyone's relief, they had a calm sea for eating dinner. In the galley there was a flurry of activity as the chef tried to outdo his own best on this, their first night out.

Everyone dressed for dinner. The men were elegant in white tie and tails, and the girls looked like flowers in their pretty pastel dresses. Rowena thought it would be difficult to find a prettier collection of young women and handsome men.

"You look lovely," Lord Patrick Tellman told Rowena meeting her in the corridor on her way to the saloon.

They had been introduced earlier that day, and Rowena had immediately been attracted by his merry talk and fun loving nature.

"Thank you," she laughed.

"You don't mind my saying so?"

"Of course not. Why should I?"

"I was afraid I might have offended you the last time we met," he said.

"But have we ever – ?" She stopped and her hand flew to her mouth.

"At the Rackingham's ball last month," he explained. "You promised me a dance and then forgot me – completely, it seems, since when Mark 'introduced' us this morning you gave no sign of ever having seen me before."

Filled with horror, she blushed as the memory came back to her.

"I don't know what to say," she exclaimed. "Yes, I do remember you now – "

"Dished," he said mournfully. "It's bad enough when the loveliest girl in the world forgets you, but when she finally says that she remembers you *now* – well, I may as well shoot myself, or emigrate – or something."

"What nonsense you talk," she said, laughing. "I'm really very sorry, and I'll make it up to you on this voyage."

"I'll keep you to that," he said with a grin.

"What's this?" Mark asked as they entered the saloon.

"I'm covered in shame," Rowena said. "Lord Patrick has reminded me that we've met before."

Lord Patrick placed a hand theatrically over his heart.

"Promised me a dance and then forgot me," he said in throbbing accents.

Mark grinned. "Miss Thornhill, shame on you! What were you doing? Deep in a discussion of fashion with your cronies, I'll be bound."

"No such thing!" she said with dignity. "I was enjoying a conversation with a Member of Parliament. We were discussing the next election. It was fascinating."

"It must have been to make you overlook this rattle-pate," the Duke said. "Now, it's time for us to go in to supper. Miss Thornhill?" he offered his arm.

"Aha, but the lady has promised to make it up to me for her cruelty," Lord Patrick said, extending his own arm.

"Indeed I did," she replied, taking his arm. "I'll be delighted to go in with you, Lord Patrick."

As they swept past, Lord Patrick gave a lofty glance at his friend and murmured, "My trick, I think."

The Duke accepted the situation gracefully, and offered his arm to Jane Stanton.

Over the excellent meal Rowena told her companion more about the purpose of their voyage.

"What we all have to do," she said, "is to enjoy ourselves. You must admit you could not find a more attractive party or a better looking one anywhere in England."

"I agree with you," he said, "and you are the loveliest of them all."

She laughed in delight. "That's just what you must say

to every woman here, so that we can all enjoy ourselves."

"I'd rather just say it to you," Lord Patrick said at once. "But since your wish is my command, I'll say the same to every young lady here."

"Good. That will start the voyage well," Rowena said, "and more importantly will make the journey romantic."

"Romantic?" the young man enquired. "But why?"

"Because we are all young and we are looking for excitement," Rowena answered. "When I think of all the thrilling places there are for us to see – "

"I think what makes the place thrilling, is the person one is with," Lord Patrick replied. "Now I am with you everything will seem more glowing than it first appeared."

Rowena clapped her hands. "Wonderful. You do it so well."

"But suppose I just want to admire you and nobody else?" he asked plaintively.

"That's not allowed," Mark said, appearing unexpectedly behind his chair. "You must work hard to spread your compliments among all the young ladies."

Lord Patrick was about to remark that he was smitten only with Rowena, but he caught a glint in the Duke's eye, and thought better of it.

Before going to bed that night Rowena went up to the highest deck and stood looking over the rail at the lights of Cherbourg.

From a little distance away she heard the sound of a man's footsteps. It would be Mark, she thought, come to mull over the first day with her.

"Good evening."

She turned, smiling. But the smile faded when she saw Dominic Fears.

"Good evening," she said pleasantly.

"I couldn't help hearing what you were saying to Patrick. It's quite some notion you and Mark have got up between you. At the same time, it is very unlikely that all your guests will fall madly in love before we return home."

"Not all of them, certainly, but even one or two would be a victory."

"Over what?"

"Over society," she sighed. "Over pushy parents."

"Oh now, there I agree. Your idea of love is charming and delightful, but does it really happen except in books? I have been disillusioned over and over again."

"What do you mean by that?" Rowena asked curiously.

"Whenever I think I've found the ideal woman she turns out to be after my money."

Rowena remembered Mark saying Dominic was very rich. She knew exactly how he felt.

"I've been disillusioned so often," he went on, "that now I make it clear to most women as soon as I meet them, that I am not the marrying sort. But with you I feel at home, because I believe you're in the same pickle."

"Yes," she sighed, "and it isn't nearly as pleasant being rich as people think it must be."

They looked at each other in fellow feeling.

"In fact," he added, "with you I think I can risk being completely frank."

"In what way?"

"I'd like to kiss you."

Rowena's eyebrows went up. "That is frankness indeed," she said. "But to be honest I only want the man I am in love with to kiss me, and I am not in love with you."

He sighed. "I was afraid of that. Do you know, you are fantastic! I never expected to meet anyone like you. I am beginning to think I would be a fool if, having met you, I lose you. Suppose I wanted to marry you?"

Rowena's lips twitched with mirth. "Is that a proposal?"

"It could be, with a little encouragement."

"After one evening? Don't be rash."

"Well, you see, you're the one girl I can be sure isn't interested in my money. That's a great attraction."

"I know what you mean," she admitted. "It makes me feel kindly towards you too. But I'm afraid it's not enough. You would have to make me fall in love with you. And that is not going to happen."

"Oh I say, have a heart. You can't be sure it won't happen."

"Yes, she can," came a voice from the shadows.

It was Mark.

"Evening old boy," Dominic said nonchalantly.

"Evening, Dominic. Goodnight, Dominic."

Dominic recognised the inevitable, and vanished.

Mark met Rowena's frosty gaze.

"My Lord Duke – " she said.

"My Lord Duke, is it? Why so formal?"

"Because I wish to complain about your behaviour. May I ask why you feel it necessary to appear like the devil in a pantomime every time a man pays me a compliment?"

"Because I'm keeping an eye on you, of course, to make sure you behave yourself."

"*Make sure I –* ?"

"I know we agreed that this was to be a Ship of Love, but I had expected you to exercise a little restraint. Instead I find you accepting attentions from two different men in a few hours, and even discussing whether you wanted to kiss a man you met only today. I'm shocked, Miss Thornhill, shocked! Have you no sense of propriety?"

"You're not shocked at all," she declared crossly. "This is your idea of a joke. Do you imagine that I am deceived?"

"No, you're fairly good at seeing through me, aren't you? Not always, though."

"And what does that mean, pray?"

"I shall leave you to guess. Shall I escort you to your cabin, or can you be trusted not to entertain any more suitors on the way?"

There was only one response to such flagrant provocation, and Miss Thornhill made it. Drawing in her breath she announced,

"Goodnight, my Lord Duke."

"Goodnight Miss Thornhill."

He bowed and stood back to let her pass. Miss Thornhill swept by him without a glance.

*

The next day they crossed the Bay of Biscay, which was choppier than they had expected. Some of the guests remained in their cabins.

But Rowena was made of sterner stuff. She was a good sailor, and instead of retiring she went up on deck, enjoying the swaying of the vessel, but taking care to hold on to something as she stood by the rail.

"Aren't you afraid to be up here?"

Startled, she looked up and saw Mark standing beside her, watching her with a little smile.

"No, I like the excitement," she said. "It's just a little blowy, but not too much."

She laughed with pleasure as she spoke. She had forgotten that she was annoyed with him.

Suddenly the deck heaved under her. Startled, she lost

her balance and was only saved from falling by the Duke's strong arm about her waist. For a moment she was leaning on his broad chest, feeling his warm breath on her neck, and her skin exposed by her low cut dress. For the first time she wondered if it was immodestly low, which was strange, because that hadn't occurred to her before.

"Are you all right?" he asked.

"Yes, I – I'm sorry." Suddenly she found she was breathless, almost as though she had been running.

"Don't apologise, it wasn't your fault." He too sounded a little breathless. "Perhaps you should go below."

"Not yet, it's so thrilling up here."

"Then hold on safely. Come further along the rail."

He moved her along to where the rail was broken by an upright, supporting the awning above them. Now she could hold the rail with one hand and the upright with the other. To make doubly sure of her safety, he placed his own hands just outside hers, so that his body made a protective wall around her.

"Do you feel safe now?" he asked.

"I feel wonderful," she cried up into the sky.

With her eyes fixed high on the stars, she didn't see the Duke's glance, half amused, half tender, just over her shoulder.

"I think we've made a good start," he said. "All our guests are so charming, some of them are bound to fall in love."

"I hope so," she mused, "and yet I wonder – "

"What do you mean?"

"You don't think we planned it too carefully? Love is something which comes unexpectedly, and not when one is deliberately looking for it. It should just happen."

"But we've simply given it a chance to happen," he

said. "There can be nothing wrong in that. But I understand what you mean. We should be careful not to try to force things. True love is elusive. I often think it is as out of reach as the moon itself, and it is something which I will never discover."

"You mustn't think that," Rowena replied quickly. "We must believe that it will turn up at any time. However hopeless it seems, love is there, waiting for us. Don't you see? We must have faith."

He smiled at her fervour.

"Of course you are right," he said quietly. "That is what we are looking for and what I believe, sooner or later, we will both find."

CHAPTER SEVEN

The sea was smoother as they sailed down the coast of Spain, and the next morning the young passengers came out onto the deck to enjoy the sun. Some of them played deck tennis, while others leaned back in deckchairs.

"I hope you're making a real effort to get to know the girls," Rowena told Mark severely. "It's only right that you should have the first pick before the other men make their choice."

"I'm doing my best, dear sister," he said. "But there always seems to be a problem. I found Dulcie charming – as long as we were discussing horses and dogs – "

Rowena couldn't suppress a giggle.

"But you know what happens if one tries to change the subject," Mark finished.

"I'm afraid I do."

"I think she and Fears will like each other. He's horse mad too. Jane Stanton I've met before, of course. She's charming, but all she really wants is to return to her fiancé. Excuse me, I see my aunt."

Lady Honoria had come on deck, escorted by Mr. Farley, and was settling herself in a deck chair. Rowena watched the charming, kindly way Mark attended to her, and reflected that there were two young women Mark hadn't mentioned, Margaret and Elaine.

Was that because they didn't interest him, or because they did?

She tried to decide which of them was most likely to attract him, the shy Margaret, or the dashing Elaine?

He could only like a really intelligent woman, she thought. And of course she must be beautiful. He's a Duke, and he knows that he's entitled to the best. Margaret's shyness might strike him as a little dull, and although Elaine is very clever, I think he could find her superficial.

Then she was surprised at herself for thinking uncharitable thoughts about her friends. It was something she'd never done before.

'But I've promised to be a good sister to him,' she thought, 'and not try to foist an unsuitable girl on him merely to stop Papa trying to match us.'

She watched as Mark went round all the girls, talking gently to Jane, then speaking to Margaret, next to Elaine, who had just finished playing deck tennis.

He spent longer with Elaine than Rowena thought was strictly necessary, and she had the strange impression that the sun had gone in.

But then he passed on to Dulcie again, who was in a bouncy mood. She accepted a cold drink and talked eagerly to Mark for some time, before bouncing off again.

Rowena wondered whether she'd been talking about dogs or horses.

Then Mark looked up, saw her watching him, and grinned. Rowena realised that he had read her thoughts and was communicating a perfect understanding.

She felt the sun come out again.

Taking a turn about the deck she came across her grandfather and Lady Honoria, heads together, chuckling.

"You two seem to be having a fine time," she said.

"It isn't only the young who can enjoy themselves,"

Mr. Farley declared.

Lady Honoria beamed.

"I'm so glad I came," she said. "You'll never guess what. It turns out that dear Adrian knew my husband when they were both young."

"Adrian?" Rowena asked. "Oh, Grandpapa."

She was so used to thinking of him only as her grandfather that she'd forgotten he must once have been young. Now she recalled that he'd fallen in love, seen his wife die and his daughter die. And that he was called Adrian.

"We studied together," Mr. Farley informed her. "Got up to some shocking larks. Our teachers said we had no business becoming clergymen, because we were too wicked. But it was just youthful high spirits."

"Jack always enjoyed practical jokes," Lady Honoria recalled. "He used to play them on me when we were married." She sighed. "How we laughed."

"I can hardly believe you're the same person who came to Haverwick Castle," Rowena said.

Lady Honoria smiled mischievously. "You know," she said, "I've always felt that if I hadn't been born into a ducal family, I should have liked to go on the stage. I'm a very good actress."

"Indeed you are," Rowena said.

She passed on, wondering what Mark was doing.

*

They finally docked at Lisbon where Dominic Fears declared he knew an excellent hotel for their dinner, and there would be an orchestra.

Everyone was mad to go, except Mr. Farley and Lady Honoria, who declared that they would have an early night. In due course hired carriages gathered on the quay, and five couples trooped off the ship to be conveyed to the hotel.

Rowena's eyes shone at the prospect of a dinner party that promised to be such fun. No chaperones, no watchful eyes, nothing to do but enjoy herself.

Her gown was primrose yellow silk, with an overskirt of white muslin, dotted with tiny yellow flowers. With it she wore opals, not her most luxurious jewels, but she was glad of that. She knew they were charming and they suited her.

As she left her cabin she found Lord Brice in the corridor.

"I hope you don't mind, I've been waiting for you," he said shyly.

"Of course I don't mind. Is there something I can do for you?"

"Just – just be my partner for this evening. Sit with me and – talk – you know."

"I'd be delighted." She liked this gentle young man a great deal.

Mark was there on deck, watching them all coming out together. He raised his eyes at the sight of Rowena and Brice.

"I see he's taken refuge with you," he said. "One of the other girls has set her cap at him, and he's running for cover. So now she'll fall to me for the evening."

One by one they went down the gangplank and into the carriages. Last of all came Mark with Elaine on his arm.

The hotel was admirable, and the food excellent. Rowena was soon deep in conversation with Brice, who relaxed in her company and displayed a gentle charm that enchanted her.

It turned out that he had been at university with Mark.

"When he invited me on this trip, I knew it would be something original and different. At college he always liked what other people either ignored or disliked. He thought and acted individually which I greatly admired."

"That is a very good description of him," Rowena agreed thoughtfully.

As the meal drew to a close, the orchestra came onto a small stage. They struck up a waltz and soon everyone was dancing. Lord Brice led Rowena onto the floor, shyly put his arm about her waist, and they began to sway to the music.

He was an excellent dancer, the best she had ever known, and she soon melted into his arms. When the first waltz ended, he asked her again and she immediately agreed. Dance after dance they had together, until at last Mark intervened.

"I think this one was promised to me," he said smoothly.

"Oh, yes – of course," Lord Brice said, becoming awkward again.

"That was quite unnecessary," Rowena fumed as she danced with the Duke.

"On the contrary, it was very necessary. You were attracting the kind of attention that I consider undesirable."

"*You* consider – ?"

"This voyage is under my supervision and I insist on proper behaviour at all times." He was really angry and her own temper rose in response.

"Well, I am not under your supervision, and I do not wish to dance with you."

She tried to pull away but he held her firmly.

"How dare you!" she whispered.

"I will not let you storm off the floor, thus attracting even more attention. And you *are* under my supervision. My authority if you like."

"I do not like, and I think you must have taken leave of your senses. Release me at once."

But his hand was tight on hers and his arm was firm

about her waist. She had no choice but to waltz with him.

"You dance beautifully," he said. "I've been watching you."

"Yes, you've been dancing with Elaine and Margaret and – "

"I've danced with everyone except you. You allowed your attention to be monopolised by one man until the whole port knows it."

"That is my affair."

"He's not the man for you, Rowena."

"Please do not interfere with my private affairs."

"Are you telling me you're in love with him? I won't allow it."

"You won't allow – ? And who are you to dictate to me? I didn't allow my father to force me into marriage with one man that I disliked, and I shall not allow you to drive me away from another man."

The music was slowing.

"The evening is over," the Duke said. "We will leave the hotel and return to the ship."

She dared not argue with him. There was a glint in his eyes that she had never seen before. He was moved by some very strong emotion, and she knew it would not be safe to cross him.

At the same time, angry as she was, she knew a mysterious thrill at the aura of danger that surrounded him. This was no ordinary man.

When the music finished he led her to the table and announced their departure. He kept her hand tucked through his arm, almost as though he expected her to make a dash for it.

They went out to the waiting carriages. The Duke handed Rowena in and got in beside her. Lord Brice gave her a forlorn glance, as though he had been hoping to sit with her, but the Duke gave him an implacable smile, and Brice immediately gave up.

When they were all back on board, the Duke gave some swift instructions to the crew, and to Rowena's shock they all sprung into action.

"We are putting to sea," the Duke informed Rowena.

"But we weren't supposed to leave for two days. We were going to see the town and – "

"I am protecting your reputation," he informed her curtly. "You may not remain in a place where you have caused a scandal."

"That is ridiculous."

"Nevertheless, it is what is going to happen."

"You're making a tremendous fuss about nothing. So I danced with him a few times."

"Seven times."

She gasped. "It wasn't seven. How can you know that?"

"Because I counted. Do you realise everyone now believes that you and Brice are madly in love?"

"And if I were, would that be any business of yours?"

He gave her a strange look. "Are you telling me that you are?"

She faced him with her chin up. "I am telling you nothing."

Suddenly his hands were hard on her shoulders. "Answer me. Are you in love with him?"

"It does not con– "

"*Answer me!*"

"No," she said after a moment. "I am not in love with him."

Something wild and uncontrolled faded from his face.

102

"Then why did you let him monopolise you all evening?" he demanded in a quieter tone.

"He's a good talker, and a very good dancer. And that's all I'm going to say to you."

He took his hands from her shoulders.

"Forgive me," he said in a jerky voice. "I should not have – I had no right to – but you must understand that I feel responsible to your father. Perhaps that has made me a little too protective of you. I ask your pardon if I went too far."

His apology, and a kind of desperation in his voice, startled her. It was impossible to be angry with a man who spoke so unhappily. Suddenly she was on the verge of tears.

"I'm going to bed," she said huskily, and fled him.

In her cabin she threw herself onto the bed, full of turbulent feelings. What had happened tonight was terrible, disturbing, unsettling. The air was singing in her ears, and nothing would ever be the same again.

"Excuse me miss." It was Jenny, yawning as she had just woken up. "Shall I undress you now?"

"Yes, thank you."

She let Jenny undo her at the back, slipped out of the dress and put on a white silk nightgown. Over it she slipped a satin and lace robe, and let her blonde hair down around her shoulders. Then she rested her chin on her shoulders, trying to think coherent thoughts, but failing.

She kept seeing Mark's wild, distorted face, full of some intense emotion that had shaken him to the core. And her.

Suddenly she too was filled with intense emotion. It bewildered her, and made her heart beat with intense excitement.

"Is it all right if I go to bed now, ma'am?"

"Goodness, I've been sitting here for half an hour. We must be well out to sea by now. Yes, Jenny, of course you can go to bed."

"Did you have a nice evening?"

"Yes, thank you."

"And Lady Honoria, did she have a nice time?"

"She didn't go out tonight."

"Oh, but she did, miss. She and Mr. Farley left the ship about an hour after you did."

Rowena turned sharply. "What? Did they say where they were going?"

"I didn't speak to them, miss. I just saw them going down the gang plank."

Rowena jumped up. Without stopping to think how she was dressed she hurried to Mr. Farley's cabin and knocked on the door. Receiving no answer she pushed it open.

It was empty.

She hurried along the corridor to Lady Honoria's room and knocked sharply. She was answered by Her Ladyship's maid, Gina, yawning heavily, and obviously just woken from sleep.

"Is your mistress here?" Rowena asked urgently.

"No, miss she said I could go to bed until she came ba–
we're moving!"

Rowena ran as fast as she could to the Duke's cabin and knocked on it as hard as she could. Then she knocked again until he opened the door.

"What the devil – Miss Thornhill?"

He quickly averted his eyes from her state of dress and Rowena realised that the satin and lace robe had fallen over, revealing her thinly clad bosom. He was in much the same condition, his shirt torn open, revealing a powerful chest, covered with dark hair.

"Something terrible has happened," she gasped.

"Your aunt and my grandfather didn't have an early night, as they told us. They went out to explore Lisbon. They're not back."

"*What?*"

"We left without them. They'll return to the quay and find us gone. They are old people. They'll be terrified."

"All right, I'm coming. Go and tell the captain – no, don't go anywhere dressed like that. I'll tell him myself."

She ran back to her cabin and hastily dressed again, this time choosing a skirt and blouse, the plainest she could find. It was no time for furbelows.

"Oh miss," Jenny said tearfully. "I'm so sorry."

"Nonsense, it's not your fault," she said briskly. "But I know whose fault it is."

Brisk and businesslike, she marched out and up to the bridge, where the Duke was conferring with the captain, who was making preparations to turn the ship.

He too was apologetic.

"Nobody knew that they had left the ship," he said, almost tearfully. "They informed nobody."

"Of course. Why should they tell anyone?" Rowena asked crisply. "As far as they knew we were here for another two days." She flung the Duke a fierce glance as she spoke, and he glared back.

She left the bridge and went to lean over the rail, watching as the lights of Lisbon gradually came into view. After a while Mark came to stand beside her.

"I gather you consider me entirely to blame for this disaster."

"Totally," she snapped. "If you hadn't insisted on leaving without thinking – "

"Why didn't her maid warn us she wasn't on board?"

"Because her maid was asleep when we returned.

Your aunt is a kindly, considerate employer who tells Gina to rest until she returns. Gina knew nothing until she woke a few minutes ago."

Mark ran his fingers through his hair.

"My God!" he groaned. "What have I done? That poor old lady, stranded alone in a strange country – "

"Pardon me, but she is not alone," Rowena said stiffly. "My grandfather is with her."

"A good man but as elderly and helpless as she is herself. They'll be frightened to death. When they arrive and find us gone I hope they'll have the sense to stay there and wait. I'll send for a doctor as soon as we arrive."

Gradually the lights became closer. The Duke had borrowed a pair of binoculars from the captain and was scanning the port. At last he said, "Ah!"

"Can you see them?" Rowena asked.

"Yes. They're there."

He handed her the binoculars and she peered through them until she saw the two old people, who had obviously seen the boat.

"They're waving," she said. "They seem to be all right."

They were doing more than waving. They were beaming with delight.

"Since all seems to be well," the Duke said, "perhaps you would like to go to bed. It's late and – "

"I am remaining right here," she told him firmly. "Because not for the world would I miss the sight of you trying to explain to your aunt why you left without her."

He flung her a withering look, but was too wise to say more.

As soon as the gang plank was in place, he was down it to throw his arms about his aunt, and shake Mr. Farley's hand, then usher them quickly aboard.

"Dear aunt, Mr. Farley, sir, how can I apologise enough – my rash impetuousness – you said you were staying aboard and it never occurred to me that you might change your minds – I will never forgive myself if you've come to any harm."

"Oh nonsense," Lady Honoria told him. "What a fuss about a little thing! We thought we'd go out and explore, and when we found you gone we knew you'd come back for us."

"At least, we hoped you would," Mr. Farley put it, and the two of them roared with laughter while Mark looked blankly from one to the other.

"He doesn't understand, my dear," Mr. Farley told Honoria.

"I know," she said. "We're old, and it offends him that we don't behave as old people are supposed to. Tell me Mark, what made you do it?"

Rowena waited for Mark to explain about her scandalous behaviour that had necessitated an immediate departure, but all he said was,

"Lisbon bored me, and I very rudely hurried on without waiting to see what other people wanted to do. Please excuse me."

"Well, I will," Mr. Farley observed. "The sight of your face as you came down that gangplank – I haven't enjoyed anything so much for years."

The two old people roared with laughter again, while Mark stood there looking sheepish. By now the others had come on desk and surrounded them, demanding to be told the night's events.

Mark took the chance to move aside and approach Rowena.

"All's well that ends well," he said, taking both her hands. "Do you forgive me?"

"Of course. But I must confess I still don't really know what you were making such a fuss about."

He stood there holding her hands and looking down into her smiling face.

"Neither do I," he said.

*

There was no doubt that the party in Lisbon had relaxed everyone on board. Now they could forget to be aloof, forget worrying about whether anyone was admiring them for their looks.

They became ordinary young people enjoying themselves with each other. The girls became soft, sweet and charming, while the men forgot they were afraid of being trapped.

They grew warmer and more affectionate to each other.

As the yacht moved into the Mediterranean, the voices grew louder, the laughter more frequent, and the atmosphere sweeter.

One evening after a merry dinner, Rowena was standing on deck enjoying the breeze and listening to the sound of laughter coming up from below. Somehow it had a strange, melancholy sound, as though reminding her that, among so many happy couples, or potential couples, she was alone.

"Don't move."

Startled, she looked down to see who had spoken, and saw Mark standing at the bottom of a small flight of stairs, just below her.

"You look like the figurehead on a ship," he said, "proud and aloof."

He came up to stand beside her.

"But what are you doing out here alone?" he asked.

"Looking at the stars," she replied, raising her gaze to the heavens, and turning slowly in a complete circle.

The Duke watched her with a faint smile, admiring her grace, and the elegant line from her chin, down her neck to her bosom. Not the least of her attractions at that moment was the fact that she seemed completely oblivious of her own beauty.

"And what do the stars tell you?" he asked.

She gave a soft laugh. "They remind me how much time your aunt spends in Grandpapa's company, and how much they both enjoy it. And then they ask me all sorts of things."

"And do they give you an answer?"

"Oh no. Stars only ask questions. You have to find the answers for yourself."

Suddenly she staggered, and would have fallen if he hadn't moved quickly to take hold of her.

"My goodness!" She put her hands to her head. "I felt so dizzy."

"It's those circles you were turning," Mark said.

"Yes, that must be it."

She stood a moment, waiting for the dizziness to subside, feeling his hands firm and strong on her shoulders. She had the strangest feeling that nothing bad could happen to her while Mark held her like this. It was sweet and pleasant, and she could gladly have stayed there for ever.

"Rowena?"

He gave her a gentle shake.

"Yes?"

"Are you all right?"

"Yes," she said vaguely. "I'll be all right. I was thinking – such strange thoughts."

109

"Tell me what they were," he said gently.

She smiled. It was directed inward, at herself, and she didn't know that it had a mysterious quality.

"I can't," she said. "They were just – very strange thoughts."

He dropped his hands. "Very well, I won't press you – for the moment. One day, perhaps, you'll want to share your thoughts with me."

She shook her head. "I wouldn't dare," she said with a touch of demure mischief. "For fear of boring you."

"Are you making fun of me?"

"I wouldn't dare do that either."

He regarded her with his head on one side.

Rowena realised that just for once she had him at a disadvantage. It was a delicious feeling. She moved away from him with almost a skip in her step, and then she noticed something on the lower deck.

"What is it?" Mark asked, noticing her sudden alertness and coming to stand beside her.

"Look down there. Your aunt and Grandpapa, strolling together again. Are we imagining things?" she breathed. "After all, everyone is allowed to love. Not just young people."

"That's very true. But I think love is flourishing among the young people too."

"Yes, it's wonderful what can happen when they feel free," she sighed. "There are so many critical eyes, so many elders disapproving of us all the time, wanting to know why we're not doing this or that – "

"Are you thinking of anyone in particular? Your father, for instance?"

"Well, perhaps. If he could see us talking like this he'd be crossing his fingers, hoping against hope that we were uttering words of love and that you'd be approaching him soon to ask for my hand."

"Yes, he would," the Duke murmured.

"And it's so nice to know that instead of that, we can talk just as friends, and nothing else, with no expectations on us, and no need even to think of love. Don't you find that a huge relief?"

"Huge," he agreed wryly.

"People say that men and women can't be friends," she said earnestly, "but I think you and I prove them wrong."

"Is that how you think of me, Rowena? As a friend?"

"Oh yes, as a dear friend, that I can trust and rely on. You don't mind, do you?"

"No, I don't mind," he said gravely, looking at her. "I'm honoured to be your friend."

"And do you think of me as your friend? No, no of course you don't." She held up her hands, shaking them slightly as though to ward off an absurd idea.

"Why do you say that?"

"Because sensible men don't need the friendship of silly little girls."

"Are you never going to let me forget those foolish words?"

"I'm not sure that they were foolish."

"I am. Very sure. I've been sure for a long time, and at this moment I think you're far wiser than I."

"Now it is you who are making fun of me."

"No. There are some situations in which women have all the wisdom of the ancients, and men flounder around making mistake after mistake."

She laughed. "I can't imagine you making mistakes, any more than I can imagine myself being wise. But I shall grow up, and learn things, and maybe, when I'm very, very

111

old, I'll be a little wiser than I am now."

"You mustn't grow old," he said quickly. "You mustn't ever be any different from what you are now. I forbid it."

The mischief was back in her voice. "His Lordship has given his orders. Can he command even that?"

"If he could, he would. But there's one way in which I can command it.

"In – " His hand stopped on its way to his heart and moved to his head instead. "In here, there will always live the picture of you, just as you are now. Young, innocent, and yet as wise as time."

He saw her gazing at him, a little mystified, and hastened to add, "Your friend will always remember you at your best. After all, that's what friends are for."

"Yes," she said happily, "that's the kind of friend I want. One who'll always think the best of me."

This was a subtle rewording of what he had said, but he let it go at that.

Below them they could see other couples strolling on the deck, young men and women, hand in hand under the rising moon. The scent of love was all around.

"This trip is going to be a great success," Rowena said happily. "I'm sure we'll have some engagements when it's over."

"And what about you?" the Duke asked. "Is the happiness of others enough to make you happy? Do you ask nothing for yourself?"

"I don't know what I want," she said with a sigh. "Except that I want Papa to leave me alone to find my own love. Or let it find me."

"It will find you," the Duke prophesied. "You were made to love and be loved. As surely as night follows day, you will find your own happiness in bringing happiness to a man."

"But I wonder who he is," she said dreamily. "Is he near or far?"

"What does your heart tell you?" the Duke asked quietly.

"Nothing. How can it, when I haven't met him yet? But I know this much – he won't have a great title. And he'll love me to distraction."

"If he loved you, perhaps you could forgive him for having a title," the Duke suggested.

She considered this.

"I'd try to forgive him," she agreed. "But it would be very hard, with Papa approving of him so violently."

"Your father's approval would count against him?"

"Goodness yes," she teased. "He must be my own choice and nobody else's."

The Duke took her hand between both his and looked steadily into her eyes.

"I hope," he said slowly, "that you have everything you want in life. I hope you marry a man who loves you as you deserve to be loved, a man who would lay down his life for you. I hope he never disappoints you or does anything to forfeit your love. And I pray that you will be happy all your days. For nothing but the best is good enough for you."

Then he dropped his head, pressed his lips fervently to her hand, and left her.

CHAPTER EIGHT

After that the voyage settled down to being leisurely and pleasantly uneventful.

But as they reached Marseilles there was an excitement of a most unexpected nature.

As the boat docked there was a cry of joy from Jane Stanton. Following her gaze, Rowena saw Frank Dillon, the man to whom Jane had been engaged, standing on the quay, his eyes searching the boat with painful intensity.

"It's him!" Jane cried. "Oh Frank, darling!"

As soon as the gangplank was in place she flew down it and into Frank's arms. The two of them stood there, locked in an embrace, while the others crowded to the side of the boat, smiling with pleasure, and exchanging knowing glances.

"Frank, Frank," Jane wept. "I've missed you so much."

"Jane, my darling, please forgive me."

"I have nothing to forgive," she said passionately. "It's all my fault."

"No, no, it was my fault for being so pig- headed."

"You weren't pig-headed."

"I was, I was."

"You weren't – "

"Why doesn't she just let him take the blame and be done with it?" demanded Lady Honoria tartly.

Mark's lips twitched. "Aunt, you have no proper feeling."

"Nonsense! I've known Frank Dillon since he was born, and a bigger booby I've yet to meet. But he has a kind heart, and if he's what makes Jane happy I'm very glad for her. I just wish they'd stop blocking the gangplank."

But when the two blissful young people came on board she was kindness itself to them. They all had to listen to the tale of how Frank had risked life and limb, tearing across Europe, desperate to reach Marseilles before the boat.

"Your parents told me you'd probably dock there," he told Jane, his eyes shining. "I arrived yesterday and met every boat. I just had to see you and beg your forgiveness for my terrible behaviour – "

"No, darling, *my* terrible behaviour – "

"If they're going to start that again I want my lunch," Lady Honoria muttered.

It soon became apparent that this was going to break up their party, for Frank had come to take Jane back to England. But how could they do something so improper as to travel alone together?

The answer was for them to marry at once, and so a service was held on board, conducted by the Reverend Adrian Farley.

Rowena led the bridesmaids, and it was to her that Jane gave her bouquet.

Then they left in a cloud of confetti, to go to the railway station, and start the journey home.

"And, do you know?" Rowena mused that evening to Mark, "I never did find out exactly why they broke it off in the first place."

"Why, because he was pig-headed of course," Mark

said with a grin. "You heard him say so."

They laughed. They were leaning on the rail looking out to sea. They had fallen into the habit of having their leisurely conversations late at night. Rowena, in particular, enjoyed them because they seemed to underline Mark's position of brother and friend.

For some reason that was important to her. She wanted to keep him safely there, because she wasn't ready to confront the confused thoughts that sometimes assailed her. Sometimes those thoughts would come to her in dreams.

Then she would see him again as he had been that night in Lisbon, his eyes wild as he demanded if she was in love with Brice, and later, at the door of his cabin, his shirt open. Then she would remember how he had seen her scantily dressed and blushing consciousness would flood her, yet with it a curious excitement.

Last of all she would recall the fervent way he had kissed her hand, which sometimes tingled with the memory.

No, she wasn't ready to confront these thoughts and memories yet. It was too sweet to drift on in this friendly companionship, knowing that later – perhaps –

"You're doing it again," Mark said, looking into her face with a smile.

"Doing what?"

"Retreating into your inner world, where I'm not allowed to enter."

He filled her inner world, if he did but know it. But she couldn't tell him, and so she smiled and said,

"Poor Jane and Frank. Why do we laugh at them, when they love each other truly, and want nothing but to be together? In fact, they alone have fulfilled the dream that brought us here."

"Even though they are a little absurd in their happiness?" Mark asked. "Let us be honest, neither of them is a shining intellect."

"Exactly, neither of them. They match each other perfectly. Why shouldn't they be absurd? Is love only for intelligent, sensible people?"

"No," he said. "You are quite right. There was something magnificent about their absurdity, because they didn't care about it, or about us, or about anything else in the world as long as they had each other."

"Because they had true love," Rowena agreed eagerly. "And it gave them the courage to be a little foolish."

"How very true, my dear," said a voice behind them.

They turned to see Lady Honoria, standing with her arm through Mr. Farley's.

"People who are always looking over their shoulder, wondering what the world thinks, are not truly in love," she said. "Everyone said I was a fool to marry my James all those years ago, but for the few years of our marriage we were glorious fools together."

For a moment her eyes misted. Then she smiled at the man beside her.

"And now," she said, "I am going to be a glorious fool again. And the world can say what it pleases."

"Why aunt, I'm delighted," Mark said, embracing her.

"I suppose I should ask your consent as the head of the house," the Reverend gentleman observed.

"You have it," Mark said at once. "I would never dare refuse my aunt anything. I'm much too afraid of her."

"Nonsense, you ridiculous boy," Lady Honoria said, giving him a light tap of reproof with her fan.

She and her fiancé went on their way to look at the stars together.

Rowena thought it sounded strange to hear Mark called a boy. After all, he was thirty, a grave and serious man. Yet it seemed to her that his gravity was less evident recently. He laughed more, and his mind seemed delightfully in tune with her own.

And now she came to think of it, an age gap of eleven years wasn't really so very much.

She met his gaze. He was still watching her with a curious little half smile about his lips, and suddenly she couldn't take her eyes away. She hadn't really noticed his mouth before. Or perhaps she had always noticed it. How wide and mobile it was, how handsome!

She wondered how it would feel if that mouth was pressed against her own. Somehow she just knew it would be gentle and tender, just at first. But then he would kiss her more urgently as he sensed her willingness, and after that –

"It's late, I must go to bed," she said hurriedly. She could feel herself blushing all over her body, and could only be thankful that in the darkness he couldn't tell.

"Yes, it's late," he agreed. "We must go to – that is – it's time to retire – tomorrow we can explore Marseilles – goodnight, goodnight."

He sounded totally distracted, and the next moment he had hurried away, without even the courtesy of escorting her to her cabin door, as he usually did.

*

They left the coast of France and began to cross the Mediterranean, heading for Kalimar, a small country on the north coast of Africa, ruled by a Sultan.

"I'm told the Sultan's a very strange character and I've wanted to meet him for a long time," Mark explained.

"Why?" Rowena asked.

"Because I enjoy people who are not exactly what one expects them to be," Mark said and then added with a twinkle, "That's why I like you so much."

"Yes, you've certainly always found me unexpected,"

she agreed with a chuckle. "Tell me some more about the Sultan."

"Very few people ever get to see him. They say his palace is quite staggering, full of gold and precious jewels."

"Will we be able to go there?" Rowena asked.

"I hope so, but I have had no introduction to him. I hope he will be impressed by the yacht if nothing else."

"Then we will hang out the flags and hope for the best. I would love to see the inside of a Sultan's palace. It will be something I will always remember, and perhaps write about in my book."

Mark stared at her.

"You are writing a book?" he asked.

"Yes, I've decided that the best way to avoid Papa's plans for me is to devote my life to literature. I'm even thinking of wearing spectacles."

"Do you need them?"

"No, but they'll make me look severe and plain."

"Nothing could make you look plain," Mark said abruptly.

"The right spectacles will. I'll choose a pair as hideous as possible, and scrape my hair back, the way you saw it once before, and when people see me they'll say, 'By Jove, that woman is so ugly she must be a genius.' And they'll buy my book, and I'll be famous."

Mark roared with laughter.

"You are simply unbelievable," he said. "But you'll have to abandon all thought of being a literary genius. Even spectacles couldn't make you look plain enough."

"Just the same I'm keeping notes of everything exciting and different on this wonderful trip. So please, please try to get us into the Sultan's palace."

"I will certainly try," Mark replied. "But I am not

making promises."

They took two days to reach Kalimar. As soon as they were there, Mark sent a note to the palace asking the Sultan for the privilege of making his acquaintance and saying his friend the Prince of Wales had spoken so often of his magnificent palace.

The response came the next day. His Mightiness, Ruler of the Sun and Moon, would be pleased to receive them. Rowena jumped for joy.

"Oh, you are so clever!" she exclaimed. "I have read about Sultans and the extraordinary life they lead, and this is a dream come true."

"You may be disappointed," Mark warned her. "The last Sultan I visited in another part of the world was a disagreeable little man. He frequently scratched himself when he was talking to me and offered me such an unpleasant drink that I had to knock my glass over, as if by accident, because what it contained was quite undrinkable."

"Let us hope the Sultan here will be different," she said.

"Well, I advise you to drink very little and eat even less," Mark warned, "however desperate you may be."

At the proper time they were collected in a carriage belonging to His Highness the Sultan. It was costly and elaborate, and the Duke could see from Rowena's face it was exactly what she had expected. But when she began to hunt in her bag he murmured hastily,

"Do not try to take notes. It will cause offence."

It was a short journey. Quite soon they could see the palace, a magnificent, turreted building, a reminder that it had once been a fortress, from which past Sultans had ridden out to slay their enemies.

They were admitted through huge bronze gates, that each took five men to open, and immediately found themselves in a garden, the most wondrous place Rowena had ever seen.

A man came forward to greet them. He was in eastern robes and had a smooth face, and an even smoother manner. He bowed deeply to the Duke, but ignored Rowena.

"My name is Ali. Great sir, His Wondrousness has commanded me to escort you to His Presence."

"Thank you," Mark replied.

"I am to tell you that he is most pleased to entertain the friend of the Prince of Wales. I am to hope that your journey has been pleasant."

"Most pleasant, thank you."

"Glorious sir, His Mightiness will be overcome with joy to hear it. Please follow me."

He walked off, still without acknowledging Rowena's presence.

"How very rude," she muttered.

"I'm afraid that in this country women don't count for much," he muttered back.

Soon her annoyance faded in wonder at the sights that met her eyes. Everywhere she looked there were archways, studded with jewels, and beyond them, ponds. In the ponds there were fountains made of gold in the shape of animals and fruit, the eyes created from jewels.

The whole building seemed to stand on archways, so delicate that she wondered how they could possibly support the weight above. Everywhere she saw mosaics, decorated with lapis lazuli that caught the sun, so that the whole place seemed to gleam.

"Oh please wait," she called. "I do so want to look at – "

But Ali was horrified.

"It is a crime of the utmost to keep His Gloriousness

121

waiting," he snapped. "Please to hurry at once." He marched on ahead. This was the first time he'd seemed aware of her existence.

Then they were in the palace, walking on smooth tiled floors between walls covered in more mosaics, also decorated with gold and jewels. The value of it all must have been fabulous, and Rowena felt as if she'd stepped into a fairy tale.

At last they were ushered into an enormous room, with dark red tiled floors.

"Magnificent," Mark observed. "Especially those tiles."

"Splendid sir, you are most observant," Ali told him. "The colour was chosen especially by our ruler's glorious ancestors, as this was the room where they beheaded their enemies." Seeing them look puzzled he added, "It didn't show the blood."

"I'm beginning to wish I hadn't come," Rowena said faintly.

"Nonsense," Mark murmured. "Think what a story it will make in your book."

At the end of the room was a dais on which stood a breath-taking throne that seemed to be made of solid gold. Behind it was a huge golden shield beneath which hung golden swords.

Down both sides of the room were lines of tall, bare chested men in dark red satin trousers. Each one had long black hair and a heavy black moustache. Each had a huge scimitar at his side.

There was a sudden blare of trumpets. A door opened at the far end, and through it came a procession. First came young girls, all dressed alike in peacock blue satin, dancing with sinuous movements. They were the first females Rowena had seen since entering the palace.

After them came male servants, bearing aloft golden dishes piled high with jewels.

Then came a wizened little man in golden robes that shimmered when he moved.

This, apparently was the Sultan, because as soon as he appeared the servants prostrated themselves on the ground. Only the armed men remained standing. Even Ali dropped to his knees.

A chair was brought for the Duke. But nothing for Rowena.

The Sultan waved for Mark to sit down, but he stayed as he was. The Sultan frowned. Mark indicated Rowena with his head.

There was a long silence.

Then the Sultan snapped his fingers and another chair was brought for Rowena.

She could have clapped and cheered for Mark.

By that time she was thoroughly out of charity with the Sultan. The gold, which had seemed so magnificent at first, now looked merely vulgar and overdone. But he would need it, she thought, to distract attention from the fact that he himself was a very ugly little man with tiny, piggy eyes, a pinched face and bad teeth.

She concentrated on remembering everything for her book. At least the Sultan would give her plenty of good material.

The Sultan greeted them, or rather Mark, in English.

"You are welcome in my country," he said ponderously. Then he stared at Rowena and boomed, "Is this your chief woman?"

"No," Mark replied hastily. "This is – this is my ward. I am in the position of a father to her."

The Sultan frowned.

"Then why do you put her on display?"

"She is not on display," Mark said. "It is part of her education to learn about other countries."

"Why? What does a woman need with education?"

Mark took a deep breath. "In England we like our women to have learning."

"Why?" The question shot out.

"It makes them more agreeable," Mark explained.

"It makes them ask questions that do not concern them," the Sultan replied. Then he leered and gave an unpleasant laugh. "Better you do as we do. Keep a woman in her place."

"That is not our way," Mark said firmly.

"I know. That is why your country is decadent. You have allowed your women to get out of hand."

Beside him Mark could sense Rowena getting ready to rise up in wrath. Quick as a flash he laid his hand over hers, holding her firmly, silently commanding her not to lose her temper. She subsided, seething.

"Our mutual friend, the Prince of Wales, came to visit me," the Sultan continued. "I asked him what he meant by allowing his mother to rule his country. Why did he not rise up and smite her?"

"And how did His Royal Highness reply?" Mark asked courteously.

The Sultan shrugged. "He said in your country a man must respect his mother. I told him it was the same in my country. I show great respect to my mother. Sometimes I even allow her to leave the palace. Closely guarded of course, but she appreciates the privilege."

"I'm sure she does," Mark said suavely.

Refreshments were served. After Mark's warning, Rowena would have been quite willing to be ignored this time, but she accepted the food and drink, just as Mark did. She took one sip and realised he had been right. After that she sat holding her glass, but didn't touch another drop.

Then Rowena looked up to find the Sultan watching her, and a disagreeable sensation came over her.

It was the slanting of his tiny eyes, she thought, and his way of looking at her as if he was undressing her. There was something gloating and unpleasant about it, and suddenly she couldn't wait to escape.

It was a great relief when the Sultan apparently decided that he'd had enough of them. He brought the interview abruptly to an end by getting to his feet. They did the same. Then he simply inclined his head in farewell, and walked out without a word, leaving them there.

"I think that was our dismissal," Mark murmured.

Guards, armed to the teeth, took up position on either side of them, and began to escort them out.

Rowena was breathing hard.

"Not a word from you," Mark warned her, "until we're well away."

In silence they walked down the long corridors and out into the blessed fresh air. Doors opened and closed behind them and at last they were outside the palace gates. The carriage that had brought them was waiting there. They climbed aboard and by mutual consent maintained their silence until they reached the yacht.

Only when they were back on board did Rowena say, "*Well!*"

Mark grinned. "I wouldn't have missed the last hour for anything. I thought you were going to explode."

"Keep women in their place, indeed! Why didn't you defend me?"

"Well you see," he said apologetically, "since we're in his country, I thought we should do things his way."

"What became of English chivalry?"

"It gave way to English common sense, I'm afraid." Mark's eyes were gleaming with amusement. "You really couldn't have expected me to take any risks in the room where he beheads his enemies."

Rowena breathed hard. Then her sense of humour came to her rescue.

"I don't see why not," she said mischievously. "With those colour tiles nobody would have noticed."

He laughed. "Rowena, you're a constant delight to me. Let's go and dress for dinner."

As they went below he added,

"I must admit I was disappointed not to see his harem, which is supposed to be enormous."

"I thought he was an ugly man and I am so sorry for all his women. I should think his breath smells if you get too close."

"Sure too," Mark agreed.

"But he was useful because I can put him in my book. He looked so villainous that he's bound to add interest, in a horrid way."

Over dinner they were regaled with questions from their guests, and between them they managed to make it sound a very funny story.

"He told Mark that women didn't need education because it made them ask too many questions," Rowena said, and everyone shouted with laughter.

"Of course a woman should be educated, so that she can be a companion for her husband," declared Lord Patrick Tellman.

"You'd run a mile from a clever woman," Margaret told him.

"That would depend on who she was, and whether she

was clever enough to be intelligent about the right things," he replied, eyeing her tenderly.

"And what would the right things be?" she demanded.

"Well, if she were cleverer than me, I hope she'd be clever enough to hide it – at least until after we're married."

They smiled at each other.

Later that night, standing under the stars, as they always did, Mark and Rowena chuckled over the day's events.

"Did you notice Margaret and Patrick?" she asked.

"Oh yes, I think they'll make a match of it. He actually mentioned marriage in public. No man does that unless he's ready for the consequences."

"We haven't really done too badly," she mused. "Jane, Margaret, your aunt. That's three brides, even if two of them – "

"Were rather unexpected," he agreed. "I think that's as much as we could hope for. The others will return to England with a new feeling of confidence. That's what really matters."

They strolled below. At her cabin door he said,

"I suppose we ought to be thinking of returning home soon."

"Yes," she said reluctantly. "It's been such a wonderful time, but it has to come to an end."

"There will be other wonderful things in life," he said softly. "Goodnight Rowena."

"Goodnight."

*

In her cabin Rowena changed into her nightgown and the satin and lace robe. Then she dismissed Jenny, and sat pensively, trying to decide what Mark might have meant by that last remark.

Suddenly she heard a sound so sad that it caught at her heart. It was like a dog whining. She stopped, listening, and the whining came again. The animal sounded in great distress.

'Someone will come for him,' she thought, but the crying went on and on.

'Perhaps it's in pain, or locked up somewhere,' she mused. 'I can't just leave it.'

She slipped quietly out of her cabin and hurried up on deck. The lights were shining on the water, and everything was very quiet and peaceful. Surely it would only take a moment to find the poor creature, so there was no need for her to go all the way back and change her clothes.

She slipped quickly down the gangplank and stood listening. The sound seemed to be coming from between some buildings. She hurried down a narrow alley until she found herself facing something that was little more than a wooden hut. The dog's crying seemed to be coming from within.

She turned the key and opened the door.

As she did so, a man's hand came out and before she could move backwards or realise what was happening, she was pulled into the hut.

There was no chance to cry for help. Two men's hands pulled her further forward and the door was closed behind her.

Then a heavy blanket was thrown over her head, and she was lifted up off the ground. Someone was carrying her away. She tried to struggle, but they held her too tightly. She couldn't even scream because the heavy blanket was pressed against her face.

She had the impression of several men, perhaps as many as four, and she knew that their strength was too much for her. Despair filled her heart. She was being brutally kidnapped and there was nothing she could do.

There was the sound of a door opening, footsteps on cobble stones, another door. Then she was roughly set down on a floor. She didn't know where she was, but it must be some kind of vehicle, because the next moment she could feel movement.

'Where am I going?' she thought wretchedly. 'What is happening to me?'

But she was afraid of the answer. She was caught up in a terrible nightmare, in which she was completely helpless. The only thing she could do was pray.

"Please God, help me! Help me!" she whispered.

She had no way of knowing how long the journey was, but it seemed endless. Then suddenly she felt the vehicle come to a standstill.

'Now I will at least know where I have been taken and what is happening,' she thought.

She felt herself lifted and thrown over somebody's shoulder. She tried to cry out, but the blanket was so thick she couldn't make herself heard. Nor could she struggle, so tightly was she held. Again she had the impression of being carried up several steps, then down a narrow passage. Then so unexpectedly that she gave a little cry, she was put down on the floor.

For the first time there were voices, speaking a strange language. Then footsteps moving away and a door slamming. She could no longer hear them.

By now she was finding it hard to breathe. The weight of the blankets covering her and the fear and terror in her own heart, made her feel almost as if she was being suffocated and would die.

It was then that the blanket was lifted off her. To her surprise she saw a woman looking at her.

Rowena stared.

Then the woman said in French, "Bonjour mademoiselle, or must I speak English?"

The last words were difficult to understand. But Rowena replied: "Where am I?"

The woman sat down on a chair beside her. Rowena became aware that she was in a large and impressive bedroom, and was lying on a bed.

The woman was staring at her. After a moment Rowena asked again: "Where am I?"

"In – the Sultan's palace," the woman replied.

She was again speaking in rather broken English and hesitated between almost every word.

"The Sultan's palace!" Rowena repeated. "Why was I brought here?"

"He thinks – you very pretty," the woman answered.

Rowena drew in her breath in horror. The Sultan – that disgusting, horrible little man – had kidnapped her.

She remembered all the things she had read about Sultans and their wicked behaviour. She remembered how he had looked at her with his dark eyes and the unpleasant way it had made her feel.

Drawing in her breath she said, "Tell me why I am here?"

The woman smiled. "Because His Highness think you pretty," she replied.

"You mean he has captured me and is making me his prisoner?" Rowena asked.

Her words came with difficulty. But already she was feeling frantic and afraid. The Sultan planned to add her to his harem, as a concubine!

Rowena pushed the heavy blankets further down her legs and with an effort sat up in bed.

"I must go back to my yacht," she said. "The Duke of

Wenfield who called on the Sultan yesterday will be very angry I have been taken away."

The woman smiled. "He not know – where you go," she said.

With horror, Rowena realised that this was true. They would find her cabin empty and have no idea what had happened to her.

"The Duke is a very important man in England," she said, trying to sound confident. "He will be very angry I was carried away in this manner."

She saw as she spoke the woman did not understand what she was saying. She therefore repeated what she had said in French.

The woman smiled again. "He perhaps – angry with you," she said in broken English, "but he not know – where you are."

It was true, she thought. How could he guess that the Sultan could do this monstrous thing?

Slowly, so that the woman could understand, she said, "Tell the Sultan I must go back immediately."

The woman laughed. "If you – tell His Highness – that," she said, "he may be very – insulted by you. You are – honoured by him thinking you pretty – and loving you."

With difficulty Rowena stopped herself screaming.

'How can I get out? How can I possibly escape?' she asked herself.

But for the moment she could find no answer.

"Now," the woman said, "you get up and dress. Perhaps – the Sultan see you."

Rowena decided that it would be wise to dress, as she would not look very dignified in her night-clothes. Her nightgown was transparent, her dressing-gown would hardly make her seem an impressive figure however angry she might actually be and however much she insisted that she should be taken back to the yacht.

"Very well," she said. "I will change into a dress but it must have a skirt not trousers."

She wondered if she was asking the impossible, for an English dress in this place. But if she wore trousers like the other women, she would seem no different, and she wanted the Sultan to understand clearly that she was very different.

She must impress on him that she was an English woman, and he was offending her country.

'I must be very firm,' she told herself. At the same time she was very frightened.

How could Mark ever think of looking for her here? Since she'd left the ship in the middle of the night, he might think she had fallen into the sea and been drowned.

She knew that only God could save her now. Desperately she shut her eyes and put her hands together.

"Help me! Help me!" she prayed. "Oh heavens, what is going to happen to me?"

CHAPTER NINE

When Rowena opened her eyes again she saw the woman coming towards her, carrying a European dress in her arms, which she threw onto the bed.

She thought the woman might be forty, or even older. She must have been pretty when she was younger. Perhaps she too had come here as a prisoner, and there was a chance of appealing to her.

"Who are you? What is your name?"

The woman smiled. "My name is Anita," she said. "I am French, and was once a governess."

Her English was jerky, as though she had difficulty in remembering.

"Then how did you come here?" Rowena asked.

Anita smiled. "I very pretty and the Sultan like me very much." She added, almost as if she was speaking to herself. "He – very fond of me – until I grew older."

"The Duke who I was with yesterday will be very, very angry that the Sultan has stolen me. He will come here and tell him so."

To her astonishment Anita laughed.

"The Sultan too clever for that," she replied. "He make the Duke believe you drown at sea."

Rowena stared at her. "How can he do that?" she asked.

"The Duke will find your shoes."

Rowena gave a cry of horror. "How would he do anything so wicked to an Englishwoman?"

Anita shrugged her shoulders. "You very pretty," she replied.

Rowena felt if Anita said that again she would scream. The other woman seemed to think that Rowena's beauty was enough of an explanation for everything, and perhaps, in this terrifying country, it was.

"And the Sultan not frightened of your country," Anita continued. "Here he is very important and visitors like you – bow to him."

Rowena bit her tongue to stop herself saying that never, *never* would she bow to the Sultan.

And she was full of despair. Now the whole horrible business was explained. How easy it would be for Mark to believe she had drowned.

'He will never think of looking for me here in the palace,' she told herself.

Anita was shaking out the dress. Rowena thought it must have come from another of the Sultan's kidnap victims.

'I have to be careful over this,' she told herself. 'I must be cleverer than they are and somehow, although I have no idea how, I must let Mark know where I am.'

She got up from the bed and let Anita help her change.

At least she looked English, she thought with relief.

"Soon His Highness will condescend to see you," Anita said. "But first I take you to the room that will be yours, and that part of the garden you can walk in."

"I would love to see the garden," Rowena replied, thinking it was perhaps a way of escape.

As they walked through the palace the surroundings changed, becoming less luxurious, more bare and plain. At last Anita stopped and opened a door.

"This – your – room," she said. Rowena stared at it in horror. It was small and roughly furnished. It had one window looking out onto a garden, but no way of getting out. In fact, it was little more than a prison cell.

"You sleep here," Anita said. "I – near you and other wives of His Highness – next door."

Rowena drew in her breath.

She was in the harem.

"You look at your garden," Anita said. "Come, see where you go when you want air."

She led the way back into the narrow passage and they passed several rooms, before she stopped and opened a door which Rowena saw led to the garden she had glimpsed from her bedroom window. Although there were a few flowers and several small bushes, the garden was closed in on either side by a high brick wall. It was at least twice the height of any woman.

She was trapped.

"You – in garden when His Highness not want you," Anita said. "Very nice garden. You breathe the air and see the sky."

She took her back to the bedroom. "You stay here until His Highness send for you. I – bring you something to eat and drink."

She departed noiselessly, and soon returned with a servant, carrying food and drink.

It was with difficulty Rowena managed to say "Thank you."

As Anita sat down on a chair beside her, she asked, "Were you kidnapped too?"

Anita shrugged.

"His Highness want me," she replied. "The French

Monsieur whose daughters I teach, believe I drown in the sea. They found my coat, my dress and my hat. What else could they think?"

"Wouldn't you like to go back to France?"

"There is nobody for me now in France. It is too long ago?"

The way she spoke and the expression in her eyes made Rowena feel with an inexpressible terror that this was what would happen to her. If Mark really believed she had been drowned at sea, he would sail away. She would not only never see him again, but she would be unable to return to England.

And her grandfather? What would he think? Would he just accept that she had drowned? But then, what else could he do?

"Soon you will become his new wife," Anita said.

"I will never be his wife," Rowena replied fiercely.

Anita gave a gasp of horror. "No, no – you not say that. Sultan very angry. Perhaps have you beaten for disrespect. But I not tell."

"You won't need to," Rowena said. "I'll tell him myself. Do you think I'm afraid of him? I'm not."

"But you must be," Anita said. "Please, it is not safe not to be afraid. For your own sake I implore you, be afraid. Show him that you respect him."

"I don't respect him, and I won't pretend to," Rowena said.

"Then you will have – very sad life here," Anita predicted.

"I won't have any kind of a life here. I am an Englishwoman, and he has no right to keep me here."

Having stated her position with more confidence than she felt, she turned her attention to the breakfast.

At last Anita said,

"Now I go see if the Sultan – ready for you."

She did not wait for Rowena to answer but left the room.

Rowena went once more to the window. But however much she looked at the walls, she couldn't see any way of climbing over them.

For a terrible moment she wanted to bang her head against the wall in her desperation.

"Please God," she prayed, "let Mark and Grandpapa realise that I'm not dead."

She heard a footstep outside and hurried back to the bed. She didn't want Anita to see her at the window and guess that she was trying to plan an escape.

Anita entered the room.

"His Highness will deign to see you now," she said.

Rowena lifted her head high and followed her without a word, striving not to appear as frightened as she felt.

Along passage after passage they walked, leaving the prison part of the building behind, before entering the luxurious part, where she and Mark had been entertained the previous day.

At last they reached the throne room, but instead of being respectfully ushered in, as before, she was stopped at the entrance by two guards carrying tall spears, which they crossed in front of her.

"His Highness will let us know when he wishes us to enter," Anita explained.

After a ten minute wait a message came from inside the room. The guards uncrossed their spears and Anita led her inside.

The Sultan was looking, Rowena thought, even more frightening than she had expected him to be. As she walked across the room, his eyes seemed to take in every inch of her. It made her shiver.

Anita curtsied low. The Sultan looked at Rowena, as though expecting her too to curtsey, but she remained on her feet, glaring at him.

An unpleasant little smile crossed his lips. With a jerk of his head he indicated for Anita to depart, and she glided away.

For a long moment the Sultan looked at Rowena in silence. At last he spoke.

"You are disrespectful in not bowing to me. For your own sake I suggest you mend your manners."

Silence.

She would neither answer nor curtsey.

"You are unaccustomed to our ways," said the Sultan in a cold, silky tone, "so I will give you another chance. You will prostrate yourself on the floor, this instant."

She met his gaze, unflinching. But she did not move.

Slowly he rose from his golden seat. Reaching behind it he removed something. Rowena flinched when she saw that it was a whip.

He came down from the dais and began to walk around her, his cold eyes fixed on her. Rowena's heart beat with fear, but she would not yield.

The whip cracked.

The Sultan aimed it expertly so that it did not touch her, but she felt it whistle past her. So that was it. He was trying to terrorise her. She gritted her teeth and did not move.

The whip cracked again.

Once more she was unharmed, but she felt the breeze, it came so close.

Her defiance seemed to drive him into a frenzy. He

cracked the whip again and again, always close to her but never touching her, while Rowena stood her ground.

Frightened as she was, a kind of triumph was growing in her. He hadn't defeated her, and he knew it. It was driving him mad.

At last he tossed the whip aside, and faced her.

"Why do you waste your time defying me?" he demanded. "It will all end in the same way, with you grovelling at my feet, begging for mercy or for love."

"Never," she snapped.

"Well, we will see who is right. But it will be well for you if you learn quickly that you are my property."

"I am not your property. I am a free born English woman, and my friends will be looking for me. You should beware of what will happen when they find me."

"Me? Beware?" He laughed. "Nobody will come looking for you. The Duke of Wenfield will quickly forget you. He thinks you are dead, and dead you are to the world of which you were part."

"If you were an English gentleman you would return me," said Rowena defiantly

"Then how fortunate for me that I am not an English gentleman. I want you! I have you! Soon we will talk. Then you will become my wife. And then you will beg for my love."

"I will never beg for your love – "

She stopped, thunderstruck by the thought that had come to her.

The Sultan had already turned away, signifying that her opinions were of no interest to him.

The next moment the guards seized her and dragged her to the door. There she was handed back into Anita's care.

In silence Rowena walked back to her prison cell. It

was a relief when she could be alone again and face the shattering thought that had overtaken her.

She would never beg for the Sultan's love, because he was not, and never could be, the man she loved.

The man she loved was Mark.

It was Mark.

It had always been Mark.

How long had she been in love with him and refused to admit it to herself?

Perhaps from the first evening when he had made her so angry, yet left her with a strange feeling of excitement. He had thrilled her even when she had thought she disliked him.

And then they had met again, in the woods, and she had sensed his power even when she rebelled against it. Her heart and her instincts had known then that the man she loved must be strong, as this man was strong.

He had proposed going away, and she had immediately found an excuse to go with him. Even then she'd blinded herself to her own feelings.

'I love him,' she whispered to herself. 'I love him. And he loves me, I know he does.'

Now that her own heart was open to her, she could see into his heart too and she found there a passion as overwhelming as her own, yet with the control and wisdom to bide its time.

She could see his eyes again, desperate in case she loved another man. She could hear the mysterious words he'd spoken to her in their late evening conversations, words she hadn't understood at the time, but which wonderfully clear to her now.

'I hope you marry a man who loves you as you deserve to be loved, a man who would lay down his life for you.'

He had meant himself. She knew that now with every

fibre of her being. The man she worshiped loved her in return, and here, in this dark, hopeless prison, she was suddenly filled with joy.

*

Anita returned in a few hours, with two other women, carrying an elaborate eastern costume that seemed to be made of cloth of gold.

"You are summoned," Anita explained. "The Sultan wishes you to wear this." She indicated the gold costume, which the women had laid down.

"I will not," Rowena said at once.

Anita gave a silent signal to the two women, who immediately seized hold of Rowena, hauling her off the bed and tearing at her clothes.

"Let me go," she shrieked, but they ignored her and in a moment had stripped her completely.

"Now you wear this," Anita said, lifting the costume.

In despair, Rowena saw her dress taken away, leaving her no choice but to put on the alien garb. As she had feared it consisted of trousers. There was a small gold satin top which covered her bosom, but nothing in between.

"It's not decent," she gasped, gazing at her bare midriff.

A shrug was their only reply. They dressed her hair and fitted onto it a gold turban, across which hooked a veil, so that the lower part of her face was covered. Then they hung jewels about her neck and around her bare midriff.

Now she looked just like a member of a harem, she thought with horror.

She tried to resist when they took her arms to lead her out, but it was useless. Two more women entered the room and they easily forced her struggling figure to go with them.

It seemed an endless journey, until at last she found

herself on a balcony overlooking the courtyard.

Looking down she saw a carriage arrive and a man descend from it.

It was Mark.

At once a hand came over her mouth, cutting off her cry of joy. It was the Sultan.

"Yes, it is your friend," he said into her ear. "He has come here seeking news of you. Now we are going down to meet him, and you will hear what I say to him. And then you will watch him depart. You will not cry out, or say a word to let him know that you are here, because if you do, he will be killed in front of your eyes. Do you understand?"

He loosened his hand and she managed to whisper, "Yes."

"Good. Remember, what happens to him is up to you."

He walked away and the two women seized her again, forcing her to follow him. She was taken into the throne room and gasped at the sight that met her eyes.

At least a hundred other women were there, all dressed identically to herself, lined up in four rows, two each side of the room. They were all on their knees, their heads bowed so their foreheads were touching the floor.

Her guards took her to a place near the throne, in the front row, and forced her to kneel with her head to the floor.

Almost at once the doors at the end of the room were thrown open. She heard footsteps coming across the red tiled floor. She did not dare turn her head, but as the footsteps neared she saw enough to recognise Mark's shoes.

He was there, within a few feet of her, and she dared not tell him. She felt as though her heart would break.

There was a fanfare of trumpets, announcing the arrival of the Sultan.

"My friend," came the Sultan's voice, "I have asked

you to visit me here because a most tragic rumour has reached me. Is it true – I pray that it is not – that the gracious lady I had the pleasure of meeting yesterday has been lost overboard?"

"The lady vanished in the night," replied Mark's voice. "Nobody knows what happened to her."

Rowena trembled. He was so close to her, yet so far away. And he sounded so sad.

"There are treacherous currents around these shores," said the Sultan. "I know that a woman has recently drowned, for my people found some of her clothes and brought them to me. Tell me, do you recognise this?"

Rowena could just make out a wisp of lace that brushed across the floor, and knew this must be the robe she had been wearing when she was kidnapped last night. And Mark would recognise it as the one she'd worn in Lisbon, when she had knocked on his cabin door to tell him their relatives were missing.

There was a total silence, as though Mark had taken it in his hands. Rowena could imagine his face, and what he would be feeling at this 'evidence' that she was dead.

The Sultan's voice was sympathetic.

"My friend, I grieve for your loss."

Mark's voice was low. "Your kindness overwhelms me. But for this I might have clung to hope for a long time."

"It is best to face a hard truth," the Sultan said. "You can begin to accept her death, and put it behind you."

"That is true. Now I know the worst, it would be better if my ship left at first light tomorrow."

"A wise decision, my friend."

Rowena felt her heart engulfed by despair. It was all over. She had nothing left to hope for.

She wanted to scream aloud to Mark that she was alive, that she loved him. She wanted to beg him to save her.

But she must keep silence for fear of harming the man she loved. Tears stung her eyes and the effort of controlling her sobs made her throat ache.

It was over. His footsteps were walking away.

Now she allowed herself to turn her head for one last look at the man she loved. As she watched the doors opened, he walked through and they closed behind him.

Stunned with grief, she let them march her back to her cell. There she fell on her bed in a passion of weeping.

"Mark," she sobbed wildly, "Mark, Mark, I love you. Don't forget me – I beg you – keep some corner of your heart for me."

But the only answer was the echo of her own sobs. Through the window she could see the darkening sky, and the cold stars overhead, massively indifferent to all human suffering.

It was all over. She would never see him again.

From now on, she would be like a dead woman.

*

Anita took her to meet the other wives of the Sultan.

This was eerie, a ghostly parody of a social occasion. Many did not speak English, but some did. They greeted her politely as the newest member of a club, and seemed to feel that she should be pleased to be welcomed by them.

They took her on a tour of the palace, which, they said, would be 'hers' as she would be the newest wife, and therefore the 'most favoured'. Clearly this was a great honour, but Rowena wanted only to die of grief.

Room after room was shown to her, so that she could be proud of her home and the many things which had been collected in it over the centuries. Rowena looked, but the majority of what she saw made no impression on her. Later when she tried to remember what she had seen, the objects which had been pointed out to her had faded completely.

All she could think of was Mark, holding her garment, and believing her dead. And her heart broke, not for her own tragedy, but for his. He would go away and live out his life without her, never knowing that she had truly loved him.

He would not know that she had spoken his name on her pillow, through her tears, and that perhaps she had died with his name on her lips.

Wherever she looked in this terrible place she saw the man she adored. While all the time she knew she would never see him again.

At last she was allowed to return to her room. They brought her some fruit and she ate it without knowing what she ate.

Then at last she was left alone, to sob herself to sleep.

*

The next day was even worse than the first one. They brought her a selection of clothes and made her try them on one after the other. At any other time the satin and chiffon would have delighted her, but now she could only think that it was taking her further from Mark.

Where was he? Far away on the sea?

The woman who was dressing her wept as she worked. Anita told her that she was a previous wife, broken hearted that the Sultan no longer cared for her. To Rowena it was incredible that anyone could love the nasty little man.

'I suppose the poor woman loves him in her own way,' she thought to herself. 'How can he be so cruel as to make her serve me? He must be a monster. I will die before I will marry him, or any man but Mark.'

But how? She thought of all the weapons she had seen on the walls, and wondered if any of the guns were loaded. And suppose she failed to die.

She thought of the way the Sultan had cracked the whip at her, and knew that would be his response to any woman who insulted him by preferring death.

At last the daylight began to fade. The other women retired, bowing low to her because she was now the favoured one, although all of them knew that the favoured one soon became no more than a servant.

Finally she was alone. She stood looking through her window as evening turned to night, thinking of Mark.

"Where are you?" she whispered. "Have you sailed and left me here? Oh Mark, Mark!"

CHAPTER TEN

They came for her at midnight. The door of her cell crashed open and Anita came in with two of the other wives.

"The Sultan is wakeful," Anita said. "He will have you now."

The other women took hold of Rowena and began to forcibly dress her in a magnificent wedding costume. Then they arranged her hair in an elaborate style. She sat there listlessly, unable to fight them. What did anything matter now?

She was marched through more corridors that grew increasingly luxurious, so she guessed they were getting closer to the Sultan's apartments. Then she was thrust into a room hung with drapes of crimson satin.

Tiger skins lay on the floor. On the walls were swords which bore dark stains, perhaps the dried blood of enemies. The atmosphere was one of magnificent savagery.

In the centre was a massive bed, covered with heavy crimson embroidered satin. On it was lying the Sultan, fully attired in his glittering robes and huge, bejewelled turban.

As Rowena came to stand in the middle of the floor, he turned his head to regard her lazily.

Then he rose from the bed and began to walk around her. He went round again and again while Rowena stood there, listless, broken-hearted.

"Tomorrow – we marry," he said, "if you please me tonight. If not – I give you to my guards."

Rowena set her chin, refusing to be intimidated by these words, although they sent a chill of terror through her. The Sultan was still walking around her.

"You're too thin," he said at last.

"Then why did you bother with me?" she asked tiredly.

He thrust his face into hers, and now she could tell that his breath was as foetid as she had known in would be.

"Because you defied me," he said viciously. "When you came to see me with the English Duke, and I had to give you a chair because you refused to be subservient, as a woman should."

"That?" Briefly astonishment forced her out of her listlessness. "But it was such a tiny incident – "

"I was forced to yield. *I was forced to yield*. That was the moment I decided to have you. From now on you will obey me. You will ask my permission to breathe. Whatever you want, you will come before me and beg for it, and if it is my pleasure I will grant it. You will rue the day you shamed me before my people."

After the brief moment of life, she had sunk back into grief.

Oh Mark, Mark!

"Did you hear me?" he hissed.

She turned dead eyes on him.

"*Did you hear me?*" he shrieked.

Then she spoke.

"You're a fool," she said.

"What?"

"You're a fool, a silly little man without dignity. The worst you can do to me has already been done, and I don't fear you. But you should be afraid, because if you touch me,

I will kill you."

"You?" he scoffed. "And how will you do that?"

"I will curse you. I will lay a spell on you that no man has ever recovered from. Every breath you take will be cursed."

She didn't know where the words came from. It was as though they poured out of her without her volition. She no longer seemed to be herself, but some other creature, who had suffered so much that she was now beyond suffering.

"If you touch me," she said, "you will be dead within a month, and nobody will know how you died."

He tried to laugh, but the sound stuck in his throat.

"Do you think I am afraid of you?" he quavered.

"Yes, you are afraid of me. And you are right to be afraid."

He tried to pull himself together. "I will have you arrested – "

"No," said a quiet voice behind him. "You won't."

Mark stood there, hatred and vengeance in his eyes.

A cry of love and joy broke from Rowena. It was impossible, and yet it had happened.

He had come for her.

The Sultan looked from one to the other, and a deep terror seemed to come over him. The words died in his mouth and he couldn't move. It was as though he really believed Rowena was a witch who had conjured up her rescuer by a dark spell.

Quick as a flash Mark yanked down one of the drapes and tore it into strips. Then he pulled off the Sultan's magnificent robe, bound him hand and foot, and threw him onto the bed.

"How on earth did you get in here?" Rowena asked breathlessly.

"I had some help." Mark indicated a man, also dressed as a palace servant who had entered behind him. "The Sultan murdered his family and this is his revenge."

"But you promised to take me with you," the man said urgently.

"And I'll keep my word."

Now Rowena noticed that Mark was dressed in servant's clothes, and looked very like the other man. He held up the Sultan's robe. "Put it on," he told Rowena. "Hurry."

"But nobody will think that I – "

"They will if you cover your face with this piece of black silk that he wears over his face when he goes out."

"Sometimes also he wears it indoors," said the servant, "because he does not like people to see his despicable face."

Swiftly Rowena donned the Sultan's robe, and his great turban. With the black silk in place she might have passed for the Sultan from a distance.

"It's lucky he's such a tiny little fellow," Mark observed. "Now let's get out of here fast," he said.

Rowena strode ahead. In front of her walked one servant, shouting the orders that made everyone fall to the ground and hide their faces. Behind him walked another servant, Mark, head down and silent.

Doors opened ahead of them, letting them through, but Rowena knew that this meant nothing unless they could get through the last door of all.

Finally they were at the great gates, and there, waiting, was a palanquin, the conveyance in which the Sultan was always carried among his people. It was like a box with open sides, on which hung silk curtains.

The gates were pulled open. The 'Sultan' climbed into the palanquin, pulled the curtains tightly around so that 'he' was concealed. The two servants positioned themselves one in front of the palanquin, one behind. They bent and lifted it.

Then they marched out of the palace and were swallowed up in the darkness.

From this incident was born a legend. The next morning a pathetic, shrivelled creature was found in the Sultan's bedroom in a catatonic state. He could neither speak nor move, and without his fine robes nobody knew who he was.

Some people claimed that he was the Sultan, and that the strange woman had been a witch who had stolen his soul, and then vanished into thin air, leaving her bridal garments in a heap on the floor.

But this nonsense was dismissed as superstition. The man was obviously an impostor, and as such he was thrown into a dungeon and left there.

The real truth, as everyone knew, was that the Sultan had mysteriously left his palace in a closed palanquin, accompanied only by two servants.

And none of them was ever seen again.

*

"You saved me, you saved me," Rowena said over and over again.

Her heart was so full of joy and relief that almost no words would come.

They had stayed with the palanquin for a few hundred yards, then stopped by the sea wall, where a horse-drawn carriage was waiting. Rowena stepped out as the men tossed the palanquin over the wall into the water.

"Ready to go?" asked the coachman.

"Grandpapa!" she exclaimed in disbelieving delight.

The servant who had helped them jumped up beside him, while Mark got into the coach with Rowena, and immediately took her into his arms. They clung together, hearts full of joy.

"You saved me," she repeated.

"Yes, I saved you," he said exultantly, "and now you belong to me."

"I thought I would never see you again," she whispered. "I thought you'd given me up for dead."

"I never believed that," he said passionately. "If you were dead I would have known, for part of my heart would have died with you. I love you so."

Then his lips were on hers in the kiss she had secretly longed for since they'd first known each other. Only now did she understand how much she had longed for it.

As the Duke kissed her and went on kissing her, she felt as if she was giving him her heart and soul. For a moment they were not two people but one.

"I have never been through such agony as when I first thought you had been drowned," he said, "and then knew instead you had been taken prisoner."

"How did you know?"

"The Sultan gave himself away by sending for me and pretending to great sympathy. Such 'kindness' from him wasn't believable. All he wanted to do, of course, was show me your robe in order to convince me you were dead. I was sure the story was false, even before I recognised you."

"You recognised me?"

"I caught a glimpse of your hair, and I knew that shining gold could only be you."

"They said they'd kill you if I made a sound."

"I guessed as much. But I knew it was you, and I swore I wouldn't let him get away with it, although I couldn't think how to rescue you. But I was given the answer when this man came after me. He promised his help if I would get him away from here. Your grandfather insisted on coming too. He said it was his job to rescue you more than mine. I said it was my job. We had quite an argument about it.

"And then, when I managed to get into the Sultan's room, I found you were managing to overcome him by your strength of will. However did you think of saying all that?"

"I don't know where it came from. It was as though suddenly I knew the one thing that could frighten him, but I don't know how I knew it. I'd prayed so hard to God to help me, perhaps that was the answer to my prayers."

They were reaching the harbour. Men ran out from the boat to help them. In moments they had all hurried aboard, the gangplank was pulled up, and *The Adventurer* cast off.

Rowena hugged her grandfather eagerly, and thanked him, but all the time she was longing to be alone with Mark. She had so much to say to him, and she was eager to hear what he would say to her.

But she knew they must wait. Everyone crowded round them, demanding to know what had happened. Rowena had to tell her story again and again, while Mark spent time on the bridge with the captain, ensuring that they made all speed out into the ocean. It was a while before they could be quite certain that they were not being pursued.

When at last he was free to leave he went below, where his aunt was waiting for him.

"I sent Rowena to bed," she said. "She was exhausted."

He nodded and thanked her, but he was impatient. There was so much he must say to her, and it seemed a long time until morning.

He knew he couldn't sleep. To get some fresh air he went up on deck.

Then he grew very still.

He wasn't alone. There was another figure there in a

pink satin ball gown, as he'd seen her once before, on that first evening.

She turned and looked at him. Slowly he came forward and took her hands.

"I should have known that I'd met my fate that very first night," he said. "You were so beautiful and full of courage. Oh my dear, my love – "

The next moment they were in each other's arms.

"I so nearly lost you," he said huskily. "Now I'll never let you go again."

He kissed her repeatedly.

"My darling Mark," she said. "It took me too long to know that I loved you."

"When did you know?"

"When I was in that dreadful place and thought we'd be apart forever. Then I had to admit to myself that you were everything to me. But it seemed too late."

"I will never let you go again," he said fiercely. "I loved you from the first moment I saw you, although I wouldn't admit it. I was so busy running away from suitable marriages, and you and I always seemed to be fighting. You were so set against me, and I had to find a way to be in your company, to get close to you and break down your hostility."

"I was never really as hostile as I appeared," she confessed. "You seemed to overwhelm me, and I wouldn't let that happen. But then you stopped giving me orders and became my friend and brother – "

"I'm a fraud, my darling," Mark interrupted. "I never meant to be your brother, only your husband. All through this voyage I've been jealous if you looked at another man. I couldn't admit to my feelings while I was in doubt about yours. But lately I have dared to hope."

"Oh Mark, we've wasted so much time," she whispered. "I want to be married to you. I love you with all my heart, and I always will."

"Yes, our love will grow stronger every day we are together. You will always belong to me as long as we both live, and after, in that beyond that we can only imagine. You are mine and I am yours, and we will never be separated again."

He kissed her until she gave a little sob of happiness and hid her face against his shoulder.

"Let us go home," he said. "And marry as soon as possible. That's all I want in the world now, to be able to call you my wife."

"Your wife," she said longingly. "How wonderful that will be! Together for ever and ever."

Beneath them the ocean stretched away as far as they could see. Overhead the stars wheeled in silent beauty.

Eternal.

Unending.

Like the love that would unite them always.